THE COLDEST NIGHT
OF THE YEAR

Ginny Vere Nicoll

❄

Feel Good Books

Published by Feel Good Books

www.feelgoodbooksonline.com

ginny@verenicoll.co.uk

First edition

ISBN: 978-0-9563366-1-3

Cover design by Tamara Hickie
(hickieandhickie.com)
from an original watercolour painting
by Ginny Vere Nicoll

The song 'The Coldest Night Of The Year'
Tobiah Thomas (www.tobiahuk.com)

Printed and bound by
KerryType Ltd, Midhurst, West Sussex, GU29 9PX

Acknowledgements

WITH SPECIAL THANKS to my daughter Tamara Hickie for a third lovely cover and to my long suffering editors, with both red and green ink! Also to Tobiah Thomas, for another alluring song! Enormous thanks go to Yassi and Paola, for helping me with the Farsi and German dialogue, to Barbara for the painstaking job of proof reading and lastly to Beccy for the finishing 'read'.

I'd like to thank Tim and his team at 'One Tree Books' Petersfield; also everybody at KerryType printers, Darren and Sue especially, for another perfectly finished novel. My thanks go to many kind people in the book world, who have kept faith and helped when, on occasion, I have lost my way.

My family and friends have remained extraordinarily tolerant of my time-consuming pastime which has meant, so often, my disappearance into another world. Marmite, my loyal little four-legged friend, is probably the only member of the family to have benefited from my long hours spent at the computer and enjoyed countless contemplative walks.

Finally I'd like to say a huge thank you to all those in the exceptionally wonderful family hotel in Saanenland, in the beautiful mountains of Switzerland, from where my story of fiction was born. It is without doubt the only place where my head clears and where I have been lucky enough to find complete and restoring peace of mind.

❄

Also by Ginny Vere Nicoll

The Smile
ISBN 978-1-4251-7153-7

Under the Olives
ISBN 978-0-9563366-0-6

THE COLDEST NIGHT OF THE YEAR

CHAPTER 1

THE little train wound its way laboriously up the mountain, exhaling a shrill whistle every time it entered a tunnel as if to emphasize its own importance. It was on time as usual and everything was as it should be: or so it seemed.

The vineyards on either side were neat tidy and the lake, already now far below, was shining and flat as a sheet of glass; the image of the hills beyond was reflected in its grey, wintry stillness. All was calm – on the outside.

The town below disappeared as the train traversed the highest pass then gained momentum as it dipped down into the next hidden valley. Snow lay deep in frozen heaps beside the track, as yet untouched by the morning sun. The one and only stop here was deserted until the smart uniformed conductor stepped down from the train to search for passengers on the platform. Not a soul in sight. The guard consulted his watch, nodded to the driver, jumped back on board and on they went again: not a sound could be heard except for the gentle rhythmic swish of the wheels rotating on the line.

There were six passengers in the first compartment and there were only three carriages for this restricted, very early morning journey. No-one spoke; all except one stared out of the window as if mesmerised by the passing scenery.

Oliver got up. He needed to stretch his legs. He'd been travelling all night. After flying in to Geneva from the USA he had then picked up the milk train to Montreux where he'd changed line once more. He was dead tired and looking forward to getting to the hotel. As he walked along the central aisle and crossed into the second and third compartments, the other people hardly even glanced his way: disinterested, too busy wrapped up in their own thoughts he decided. Perhaps they also had been travelling through the night. The rest of the train was empty. There was nobody else on board; just eight people which included both the conductor and of course the engine driver. An expensive journey for the company, Oliver supposed, hence only the three carriages.

The train slowed as it entered another long dark tunnel, lurching slightly as the brakes were operated when they negotiated a bend on the narrow-guage track. The scream of the whistle echoed eerily. Then, unexpectedly, the train came to a noisy, shuddering halt. The machinery suddenly stilled, clicked and sighed, as if protesting at the sudden inactivity. Oliver sat and listened: there were places on the line where two trains were unable to pass and so, he remembered, periodically there were these unscheduled stops for one or other train to calculate their timing accordingly.

There was the suggestion of a slight commotion somewhere up front. Then a door swung shut and relative silence resumed once more. It was a strange feeling to be seated alone in the vacant carriage waiting to come out into the light again. He could almost imagine the ghosts of passengers from by-gone days, sitting quietly beside him: a cold shiver ran down his back. He shook himself free from the melancholy; strange thoughts for one about to join his girlfriend, on holiday in the mountains, mused Oliver. He must be very tired. Minutes passed, then with another jolt they rattled on again towards their various destinations.

Oliver returned to his seat and sat scrutinizing his fellow occupants. Two were sitting with their backs to him, one a grey haired older man now intent on a newspaper, the other a well groomed woman, of uncertain age, whose head was turned towards the window. Judging by the little he could see of her he thought that she was most likely attractive. He waited, hoping that she might turn around so that he could be proven correct in this assumption. The other two people were facing him. Both were younger men, about his own age, he guessed. They appeared not to be together as neither spoke. Both looked uncomfortable, almost ill at ease for some reason and he very much hoped that neither would be joining him at his hotel. They wouldn't make the most exciting dinner companions.

He turned to look out of the window, catching a distorted view of his own dishevelled reflection at the same time. The road ran along side them for the moment. Cars and a white van easily overtook them giving the illusion of great speed, but in fact it was only the lethargy of the little mountain train that made it appear so. Oliver leant nearer to the window and peered more closely at himself again then sat back, thankful that he could see so little detail. He closed his eyes for a moment running his fingers across them and up through his hair. His eyes felt gritty and his head tender to the touch with tiredness. It shouldn't be long now. Olly was longing to get there. He mustn't go to sleep and miss his station. He thought of his delectable Rose meeting him, followed by a hot bath, room service and then bed. Immediately he began to feel better and more alert.

Oliver opened his eyes with a start. There was something odd here. What was it? His weary brain was struggling to focus. He looked again at the passengers, studying each one in turn. Suddenly he realized: there should have been six people, including himself in the carriage, but now there were only five. One had disappeared. Oliver spun round, looked behind him, then stood up. Nobody: there was no sign of the sixth person having changed seats and no-one had passed him by.

He knew that the one and only lavatory was unoccupied; he'd just walked back past it and the door had been open. He'd noticed in particular how immaculately clean it had been.

He concentrated hard trying to remember where the missing person had been sitting and what he looked like. Yes: it was a man of swarthy appearance who'd been wearing a rather old-fashioned grey duffle coat, sitting alone on an aisle seat facing him. The coat seemed unusual in this day and age, well loved and well worn; certainly vintage, he had noticed it especially. So Oliver certainly wasn't mistaken. But where was the man in the duffle coat?

He was wide awake now puzzling the situation. He'd go for another walk right through both other compartments and, if there was no sign of the man, then there could only be one explanation; the duffle-coated person must be a local, known to the driver or conductor and he'd be up there in front, talking to them, exchanging family news. That was the obvious answer, but really it was none of his business anyway.

Walking back through the unoccupied part of the train Oliver decided that exhaustion really could induce paranoia; but perhaps, in his case, it had something to do with the film he'd made the great mistake of watching on the plane. He had thought it unnecessarily blood thirsty, particularly when people mostly wished to be lulled to sleep, as they winged their way out across the Atlantic.

Having reached the end of the train Oliver turned, walked back through his own carriage, through the sliding door and on into a small goods area which backed onto the engine driver's cabin. He could clearly see that there were only two heads behind the tinted glass: there had been six passengers and no-one had moved at the last stop.

The conductor appeared from out of the cabin to see what the young man, standing waiting, required of him. Oliver attempted, in German, to explain about the missing passenger. The Swiss railway man merely shook his head and muttered his apologies, for not understanding, or perhaps pretending not to understand him, Oliver thought unexpectedly: he also tried French but to no avail and then gave up altogether. This, he came to the conclusion, was definitely one weird situation. He smiled at the man who it seemed couldn't quite meet his eyes, indicated there was no problem and returned defeated to his seat.

*

Rose was excited: Oliver would be here soon. She decided that she had time for a quick walk before going to the station to meet him. It was cold and there was plenty of snow for skiing. She just couldn't wait for tomorrow, when they would collect their skis and get out onto the slopes together. Today would be for catching up and relaxing; spending quality time and for romance. Putting on her fur boots and wrapping a scarf around her neck she grabbed her coat and gloves then, with one last look to see if the room looked reasonably tidy, she shut the door and ran downstairs.

Hélène looked up from behind the reception desk, taking pleasure in seeing the blatant excitement etched clearly on Rose's vibrant face. The young English girl wearing her big cosy snow boots jumped down off the last stair and landed softly in front of her. She was dressed in a warm emerald green jacket, the hood with fur around the edges framed her arresting features. In places her dark unruly curls had escaped.

Rose looked a little like a very attractive but rather naughty school girl, thought Hélène amused; vivacious and full of fun. She and Oliver came every year. They were popular guests. Hélène and her family liked them both very much.

"Hello Rose! Are you going for a walk? Isn't Oliver due to arrive soon? You'd better not be late or you'll be in big trouble!" She laughed flicking back her own long dark hair as she did so.

"No, no! Don't worry. I won't be late. I know what time to expect him. I'm just going to whiz out for half an hour first to get some air before meeting him. Do you think I've got time? He gets in at nine fifteen." Rose glanced at her watch doubtfully. Hélène looked across at the old grandfather clock opposite her.

"Yes, you'll be alright but don't go too far; maybe up to the bend, half way to the middle station, would be a good distance. You'll see the train from there, approaching along the bottom of the valley. Keep to the pisted track above and you'll recognize the quick cut down from there?"

"Yes, I'll remember it. Thanks Hélène, see you later then! Bye!"

Rose ran out of the door in a flurry. The head housekeeper came down after her, carrying a load of linen. She was smiling.

"Maybe this year?" she enquired of Hélène inclining her head towards the door with obvious meaning.

"I hope so," came the reply, "I really do hope so Ingrid; they are such a lovely couple."

*

Rose walked quickly up the hill puffing slightly with the exertion. Mountain air was thin. She had only been here for two days, having flown in from a business trip in Paris; an interior design trade show and, as yet, she hadn't quite acclimatised. Besides which the walking wasn't easy with either icy snowmobile tracks to follow or large piles of snow to negotiate in between the ruts. It had really dumped it down in the night. The trees were laden and the sun, now up, sparkled onto a pure white vista. Rose stopped for a minute to admire the breath-taking view before her. She could see the train line below and shading her eyes could follow it, all the way along the valley, as far as the next village. She also knew that she would hear the train whistle as it approached the station, so would be warned of Oliver's imminent arrival. Her stomach churned with excitement and anticipation. Soon they would be together again and for two whole weeks.

At the sharp left hand bend in the road, which then wound on up to the 'middle mountain ski station', Rose set off turning right along the track. It hadn't been cleared and the first few steps, in the virgin snow, were nothing short of exhilarating. Nobody else had walked this way today. It was both too early and too cold.

Rose tramped on through the thick snow, marvelling at the bird and animal tracks criss-crossing the winter landscape. The cold air stung her cheeks and her boots made a soft, scrunching, squeaky noise as she walked: so satisfying. She dug her hands deep inside her pockets. She'd put her gloves down somewhere in the hotel and forgotten them when she'd left in such a hurry, but she wasn't cold: the exercise, air and Oliver's expected arrival was just too intoxicating to feel anything but absolute happiness. Rose checked her watch: only about ten minutes to go. Now somewhere shortly, as Hélène had said and if she remembered correctly, there should be a short cut down to the station. The timing would be perfect.

There had been so much snow that the short cut wouldn't have been easy to find but for the fact that there were some footprints, coming out from behind some bushes onto the path, a little further down. There was a circular, trampled area in the middle and it looked as though something big had been dragged some distance. Rose moved nearer, peered more closely, then stared in fascinated horror as she recognised what had actually drawn her attention. There was a large area of it with spatterings to either side. The patch had sunk a little as it froze, but there was no doubt about what it was and in contrast the colour was shockingly vivid. There was blood in the snow.

Rose looked up, then down again, as if mesmerised. An animal: it had to be an animal. But there were no four-footed markings. The prints were definitely human. There must have been an accident, thought Rose. Hélène had said nothing but maybe she hadn't heard yet. Rose looked for further footprints, but at the far side of the circular area they appeared to have been wiped out. There were only signs of what appeared to be a large sleigh or something similar, progressing downhill. Any other marks had been completely obliterated by the heavy sled. Well! There had to be a reasonable explanation, thought Rose, but what an unexpectedly horrid start to the day. The poor person involved in the accident must have been badly hurt, judging by the amount of spilt blood.

She was distracted by a distant short, sharp, whistle blast. The train was approaching. It was time to go, so she stepped carefully over the offending blood, picked up an oblong bone coat button which she had noticed near the bushes as she passed and, stuffing it in her pocket, went hurriedly on her way.

❋

True to the efficient Swiss rail system the little train had made up the time lost in the tunnel and slid gently into the station at nine fifteen precisely. With an exaggerated hiss the doors opened and out jumped a grinning Oliver. He dumped his case on the ground and looked up just in time to open his arms to Rose who hurtled into them.

"Oh my God Olly. You're here; you're here. I can hardly believe it. I'm so excited," she cried.

"Keep still for goodness sake!" replied Oliver kissing her soundly then holding her away from him to look at her properly.

"You look wonderful, all pink cheeked and sparkling. Now what exactly have you been doing without me these past two days?" he teased, hugging her.

"Well, you're not going to believe this, but actually I've got rather a lot to tell you..."

"Good, then let's not stand here any longer. It's cold. We'll go on up to the hotel," Oliver interrupted, noticing the slightly querulous voice and an anxious expression fleetingly touch her face.

＊

In their bedroom, other matters temporarily put to one side, Oliver concentrated on persuading Rose to join him in the shower. She giggled.

"But I just had one and washed my hair less than two hours ago," she protested feebly.

"Who cares?" replied Oliver, "we're on holiday and I'll help you dry it this time." Then he systematically began to undress her and again bent to determinedly kiss her. Rose uttered a sigh of resignation and happily gave in.

Some time later Oliver sat up full of energy once more and hungry. He looked down at the sleeping dishevelled Rose sprawled in bed beside him. She lay on her side facing him; one long slender arm crooked, with her hand tucked under her chin. Her dark eye-lashes lay softly on her cheek; the few freckles, on her up-tilted nose, appeared distinctive on her skin, pale now in tranquillity.

He adored those freckles which, on occasion and against his wishes, she tried so hard to cover. Her naturally curly hair was more rumpled than ever after their rampant and most satisfactory love making. He loved her completely and utterly. They had been together two years now. Perhaps it was time to change things and this holiday could be the perfect opportunity he thought.

Oliver gazed out of the window, enjoying this quiet moment he had to himself, luxuriating in his present situation. Two whole weeks off with the girl he loved: what more could he ask for? Work-wise recently they had both had quite a bashing, holding down two very demanding jobs. His highly paid and stressful City position necessitated much travelling and appalling hours which was not ideal for any on-going relationship. Rose's interior decorating business also had lately taken off to such an extent that her clients all came in a rush, requiring everything to be finished at the same time and in an impossibly short time, putting Rose as well under a lot of needless pressure.

Not wishing to disturb her, Oliver stretched carefully then considered the rest of the day ahead. With a jolt he remembered his strange journey on the mountain train and the disappearance of the duffle-coated mystery man. He turned again towards the sleeping Rose. She was now beginning to stir. In view of the worry the family had been experiencing over her older sister with her traumatic medical problems, Oliver decided to say nothing, at least for the moment.

Rose half opened her eyes and smiled. How very lucky she was. She yawned and held her arms out remembering that he was here at last.

"I suppose you're going to tell me you're hungry?" It was a statement as much as a question, but she knew him well. He nodded and ruffled her hair, grinning.

"Yes, come on, it's nearly lunch time and unlike some I didn't have any breakfast!"

"OK, OK point taken. I'll get up. Where shall we go?"

"Let's stay here in the hotel. I need to say hello to everybody. We can sit outside on the terrace if it's warm enough and then perhaps go for a walk afterwards. What do you think?" A cloud flitted across her face. Oliver frowned catching her eyes.

"What's wrong, my darling?"

"Oh! I don't know. It's probably nothing. Just me being a little paranoid I expect and reading or watching nerve-racking thrillers too late at night..." she hesitated, "Anyway I'll explain over lunch."

They dressed, went downstairs and into the dining room. Oliver began to greet the staff while Rose held back: she'd seen Hélène through the open door of the office. She went across and politely knocked on the door.

"Hélène, I'm sorry to disturb you but... may I ask you something?" Hélène looked up, stopped working on her papers, got up from her chair and came to the door smiling.

"Of course. I am pleased to be distracted from this horrible work! There is so much extra, I'm so behind after the drama last week. I've no doubt that you heard about the cable car breaking down?"

"Yes what an awful thing with all those poor people being stuck for so long," Rose replied sympathetically. "I'm so glad that nobody was hurt."

"No, thank goodness, but we were turned into a soup kitchen. The hotel became the base for rescue operations, so we couldn't do much else except look after a lot of very cold people! Never mind I'm catching up now. How can I help you Rose?"

"Well, it's just that I need to ask you something... um... was there any sort of accident up near the middle station this morning, early or even late last night? I'm sure you would have heard by now if there had been."

Hélène looked puzzled, but answered immediately shaking her head.

"No, no... not as far as I know; what sort of accident? What do you mean exactly?" Oliver was approaching.

"Oh look! Here's Olly coming to say hello... It's okay, don't worry Hélène, it was obviously nothing." Oliver was holding his hand out.

"Hélène, hello! How wonderful to see you again and how is Anton?" he kissed her, three times, according to Swiss custom. "You have no idea how great it is to be here, just like returning home." Hélène laughed.

"Good. That's just how it should be. It's lovely to have you both here once more. Anton is good, thank you, and he'll be here tonight. Now go and have a good lunch and relax, unless you'd like to come in here and help me with this lot," she gestured despairingly.

"No thanks," replied Oliver, moving away, feigning horror. "We'd rather go and make sure that Ramon's cooking is still up to scratch. See you later!"

*

They sat outside, in a sheltered corner, on the terrace. The sun was strong and both needed their sun glasses. Oliver ordered a bottle of Suisse Fondant wine while they perused the menu.

"I'm starving," he said. "All that travelling and extra activity on arrival," he winked at Rose, "however I'm going to keep it light so that I can walk in this wonderful snow and also have plenty of room for dinner later. What about you, my darling?"

They both chose soup, pasta and salad then, the order given, Oliver removed his glasses and took hold of Rose's hand across the table.

"Right now... we have only been apart for a week. I rang your mother from Heathrow so, for the moment at least, all is well with your neurotic half sister. Now we are together in this most idyllic place, which we both love, so tell me Rose: what could possibly have happened here to upset you? What on earth is wrong?"

* * *

CHAPTER 2

OLIVER was having trouble keeping up. This hill always seemed steep for the first few days and they'd polished off a whole bottle of wine for lunch which always made him sleepy in the middle of the day. Actually, he would have rather liked another sojourn in the bedroom, before setting out on this particular wild goose chase. In his opinion, someone had obviously been out after rabbits or something furry and good for the pot. But it was no use arguing. Rose was determined to show him where some heinous crime had been committed.

"Rose, for goodness sake, can't you slow down? There's really no rush. It's minus six out here, so the evidence isn't exactly going to melt."

"Yes, there is a hurry. It might have gone or been removed by someone; then you'll never believe me."

"OK, but just wait a bit and let me catch up. I'm puffing like an old grampus."

Rose stopped and turned around to wait, a look of affectionate apology on her face. She held out her hand.

"Sorry Olly! I'm sorry, really I am. It was just such a shock, coming across all that blood and… I want you to put my mind at rest; then we can forget the whole thing."

"It's alright. Come on then, I've got my breath back so… where is it?"

At the bend in the road they turned off, onto the track, just as Rose had earlier. Now there were two more sets of footprints in the snow, one pair either side of Rose's boots, which had conspicuous ridging underfoot.

Nothing unusual about that, thought Oliver: many walkers took this track which continued all the way to the next village. Rose was ahead now, almost at the place she'd described. She hurried down the beginning of the cut, then stopped dead, gesticulating frantically.

"It's gone Olly, it has gone," she shouted. "Someone's cleared it all away. Look! I can't believe it."

Oliver hurried to her side. She was right. Someone had indeed rather roughly pisted the little path. In the past nobody had ever bothered to clear this particular route which was too small to merit enough use either by locals or hotel guests.

Rose appeared distraught, so Oliver decided to take charge before the incident was blown out of all proportion. He stood beside her and putting an arm around her shoulders said gently:

"Alright now, explain to me again exactly what you saw here this morning." Rose described, in detail, the whole harrowing scene, just as she'd seen it. Then she took her glove off and delved into a pocket, rifled around and pulled out the button she'd picked up earlier, near the bushes.

"I found this button, right over there," she gestured with her arm. Oliver's eyes followed to where she pointed, then back to her hand.

"The button has been torn off quite violently. It's actually got a piece of coat still attached. Look!" she held it out. Oliver inspected the offering. The button was traditional, oblong, made of bone, and the torn piece of cloth was grey.

Alarm bells began ringing: thank God he hadn't yet told her about the missing duffle-coated person on the train. The small piece of grey cloth and button appeared similar to the garment worn by that elusive man.

"Stay there for a minute. I'll just have a look around," Oliver said as he stepped carefully off the path where other prints appeared to have joined it, coming from the direction of the thicket. He walked over and lifted a branch, then bent to peer underneath; the bough promptly distributed its heavy load of snow all over his back. On any other occasion Rose would have seen the funny side and laughed.

The acrid stench hit his nostrils first. Then he saw the reason for the smell: there, on the ground, completely protected from the winter wonderland outside was a lethal, rusted metal trap. Locked firmly between its cruel jaws, its eyes wide with terror, even in death, was a poor unsuspecting Alpine marmot. The wretched animal's life blood still seeped away into the ground beneath. It couldn't have been long dead.

"What is it? What have you found?" called Rose in an unsteady voice. Oliver dropped the branch and stood up to shake himself, smiling and somewhat relieved. He had to admit he had begun to imagine macabre goings on himself.

"It's alright, the mystery is solved. I'm afraid someone's been out trapping. It's a dead marmot. I expect what you saw this morning was the blood of a deer or a hare, at any rate something bigger than this."

"Oh Olly, thank God for that. I really did think that someone had been murdered."

"I know you did, silly girl," he said, "but it really isn't very likely that anyone is going to be done in around here, you know. However I think that we should report the trapping. I'm sure it's illegal; otherwise the people responsible wouldn't have bothered to cover it all over. Come on, it's freezing standing around here, let's go back for some hot chocolate." Arm in arm they set off once more, happy in the outcome of the investigation and thrilled to have two whole weeks off, in each other's company, with no work before them.

"I still think it's a bit odd that this particular path was cleared, for the first time, this very morning and I can't really believe that mere poachers would take quite so much trouble," mumbled Rose, but he didn't hear.

Oliver had left the path and was busy making a snowball and he didn't usually miss when he threw them either. She ducked just in time then ran giggling to hide in safety behind a tree. This game of 'duck and miss' could continue for some time.

❄

The sun went down, leaving behind a spectacular, glowing, pink sky over the cold landscape. Grey clouds scudded hurriedly across heralding perhaps more snow to come later. Then day merged quietly into night. Together, on the second floor, Oliver and Rose gazed out of their bedroom window and watched the little roof lights flick on all around the village, below the hotel.

"It really is a Christmas card scene isn't it?" said Olly. "All we need is sleigh bells and Santa in the sky."

"That's not like you to be quite so romantic," replied Rose amused. She turned to appraise the tall, slim man beside her. His hair appeared darker than usual after the shower he'd just had, and his grey eyes were twinkling. Those eyes could appear quite steely, she remembered, when he was cross; but that wasn't often.

"No...? well, you make me feel romantic, come here!" He made to grab her, but she backed away.

"No, no! Olly, not now, not again, I'm ready for dinner," she protested, laughing. He raised and spread his hands in mock resignation.

"Sorry! OK, don't worry, I won't mess you up… anyway I'm hungry for food now and it's time to go down, but you won't get away with it later, of that you can be quite sure." She smiled at him somewhat ruefully and moved to the other side of the room so that he could inspect her newly-acquired French clothes.

"What do you think?" she asked, twirling around, her dark eyes bright.

Oliver stood back admiringly, taking in every detail. Rose had on a dark grey pair of trousers, with a wide belt, which fitted her slim boyish figure to perfection, and an immaculate white shirt sporting the lapis cufflinks he'd given her for her birthday, which also matched her earrings. Over her shoulders she wore a fringed grey and white alpaca shawl which he'd seen before. To finish the outfit she wore black, high heeled, suede boots and carried a small clutch bag of the same fabric. Her thick curly hair, as usual, was rather out of control and the little make up she wore merely enhanced her own healthy colouring.

"Rose, you're a one off," Oliver said appreciatively. "You look completely and utterly delectable and I'm the luckiest man alive. Come on, let's go down or I shall have to break my resolution right here and now."

✳

The four friends sitting at the bar noticed the good looking couple walk past them into the dining room.

"That's the other English couple that Hélène said we'd like so much," Alicia informed the others. "She and I met in the ski shop yesterday. He's only just arrived."

"You seem to know a lot about our fellow guests, but they certainly do look nice enough," replied her husband Guy with obvious meaning, winking at his friend on the bar stool beside him.

"Yes," agreed Julian, "I'll bet she really bombs down the slopes: great legs!"

"Honestly you two, you are incorrigible, anyway I'm going to say hello again when the occasion arises. I'd like to get to know them."

"You never know, but after a couple of weeks out here, we might all end up life-long buddies," agreed Adriana, backing up her friend. "Now you guys, how about dinner or are we going to sit here all night?" She stood up, tossing a mane of tawny hair, her hazel-coloured eyes shining mischievously.

"And what's more," continued Alicia, the cooler blonde of the two, "we might like them so much that they could even end up becoming God parents to our first child; when I'm allowed to have one, that is," she added bending down to her husband, kissing him on the ear and stalking off. Guy looked slightly taken aback.

"Also…" Adriana chipped in, glancing back over her shoulder, "I hear there's a devastatingly 'good news' doctor arriving tomorrow and he's on his own; so you'd better look out, you two!"

"Well my lad, that's you told then," laughed Julian. "It's family now, is it?" Slapping his stunned-looking friend on the arm, he jumped off the stool and followed the girls into the dining room. Guy thanked the barman, who by this time was also discreetly chuckling, and moved off after the others, mumbling to himself.

'Oh dear, this baby business was becoming alarmingly serious.'

Dinner, as ever, was excellent, with numerous beautifully presented courses, washed down with copious amounts of light Swiss wine. Rose met Alicia and her friend at the salad bar, where everybody was expected to help themselves. Rose had spilt all the croûtons. With much amusement, the other two helped her scoop up all the little fried bread cubes before anybody else noticed. Thus was the beginning of what was to become a firm and enduring friendship.

*

The hotel dog planted himself determinedly on the floor beside Rose. His head lay across one of her feet. He was a black Labrador and had been part of the family for as long as she and Oliver had been visiting the hotel. During dinner the rest of Hélène's family stopped by each and every table to introduce themselves to strangers and to say 'hello' to old friends. Nobody was ever left out. The hotel was meticulously well run and the atmosphere one of delightful tranquillity and comfort. After all, the large majority of people were relaxing on holiday. Rose and Oliver sat for a long time, cherishing every moment of their first evening, until the staff began surreptitiously clearing the tables around them.

"They need to lay up for breakfast, so let's go and have a nightcap at the bar," suggested Oliver.

They moved together out of the dining room and along the passage towards the main door. The hotel bar entrance was to the right of the front door, opposite the reception desk. Some people in front of them were putting on their coats before leaving. Probably local people or friends of the family, thought Rose, more interested in anticipating a glass of Cointreau. There was a rush of cold air as the group started to exit. Oliver, close behind her, stopped suddenly. The man just leaving, who had shot him a furtive glance, was familiar.

"Hang on a minute," he said as he pushed past Rose and followed the man out through the double doors.

"Excuse me, I'm sorry but are you...?" the man in the duffle coat spun around, a look of surprise and perhaps slight alarm etched on his swarthy face.

This individual bore no resemblance whatsoever to the one on the train: this one, although also Middle-Eastern looking, wore a small goatee beard. Oliver excused himself, apologising profusely. The surly look-alike wasn't in the least bit amused and turned away to stalk off on his own. Oliver rather embarrassed hurried back inside, out of the cold, and returned to Rose's side. She was looking suitably bemused.

"What on earth were you doing Olly?" Oliver managed to smile reassuringly.

"I just thought I knew someone, that's all. Forget it, let's get that drink."

"All right, I'm just going to wash while you order. I'll be right back."

Oliver headed on towards the bar, uneasy for some reason. Why should he feel so strongly about that man, who wasn't the one who had disappeared on the train anyway? But he wore exactly the same unusual coat which was a bit odd in itself. However, it was more than that – the man looked completely out of place and gave off an overpowering sense of hostility when approached in a holiday hotel exuding comfort and contentment. Strange – the man had something to hide, thought Olly. Of that he was sure.

As Rose came back past the office Anton was shutting up for the night.

"Hello Anton. Were those local people who just left? Olly thought he knew one of the men."

"Oh! Hello Rose. No. Actually I haven't a clue; they weren't all one party. I've never seen any of them before. I think they came from Zurich. We do get quite a lot of business people passing through and they didn't all seem quite like holiday makers, did they? Did you have a good dinner? I hope you were well looked after."

"It was, as always, a delicious dinner thanks," replied Rose. "Now we're just going to have a nightcap before Oliver keels over with tiredness. I really can't imagine how he's still standing after all that travelling."

Rose joined Oliver at the bar. She thought he appeared pensive, just for a moment, before he heard her approach. But he was soon his usual ebullient self. Where did he find the energy? She would have been dead on her feet.

They didn't stay long and after waving to the two English girls and their men, sitting at a corner table by the fire, they soon made their way upstairs to their room. Rose kicked off her shoes and, grinning, leapt onto the large double bed. Oliver watched her, a smile spreading quickly across his face.

"It's very comfortable here," Rose announced patting the place beside her, "good springs... and there's plenty of room..." she began jumping up and down, at the same time enacting a comical strip tease, as she began to wriggle out of her trousers.

"Plenty of room! For what, might I ask, you wicked girl?" interrupted Oliver taking off his shoes and landing on the bed in one bound.

"Come here. You really are indecently sexy and funny too. Now stay still, I'll help you take all your clothes off."

"No, it's too cold," giggled Rose, dropping down and diving under the duvet cover.

"Don't worry about that," replied Oliver, starting to take off his own clothes, "I'll soon make you warm. I want you so badly... shan't be able to wait long."

"Doesn't matter. We have all the time in the world, two whole weeks. Hurry up." Rose disappeared again down the bed.

Oliver stripped off his own clothes and when next she peeped out, from underneath the duvet, he knew she'd done the same. Fuelled by wine at dinner, a joy for living and in each other, with blissful abandon the lovers let their natural instincts take control. Thrilled to be together again, they rolled beneath the covers, enveloped in an all-consuming and exhilarating physical need. The boisterous laughter soon subsided as united they concentrated in climbing together up towards the blinding light of that ultimate sensation, paused at the brink to relish the dizzying point of no return then, with triumph, tumbled down the other side into the timeless wonder of it all.

❋

It was sometime around dawn that Rose awoke with a start. That was it. She knew there had to have been a reason for Olly's odd behaviour when he'd run out of the door after the departing guests last evening. But she'd missed it: it was the coat. One of the men leaving was wearing an old duffle coat. She hadn't fully absorbed the information at the time, wondering instead what Olly was doing rushing out into the cold night air. But now she realized that it was most likely the garment would have had buttons on it just like the one that she'd picked up and shown to Oliver, near the frozen blood. Even the colour of the cloth was the same. So Oliver hadn't dismissed the whole saga as she had thought. He had believed her story after all. Besides which, the elusive chamois never ventured near the village. The animals were far too shy and only inhabited the very highest ledges of the mountains. She knew perfectly well that there was far too much blood in the snow for it to have been a hare.

❋ ❋ ❋

CHAPTER 3

SUNDAY morning. Rose had suffered a restless night, finally sleeping only in the early hours, then awaking late, well after sun up. Oliver was in the shower; she could hear his rather tuneless whistle. She lay luxuriating idly in the large bed, knowing that it didn't really matter what time they went downstairs; breakfast continued until eleven o'clock. They could start the day slowly and almost have the slopes to themselves while everybody else was lunching. After a cooked breakfast, a simple bowl of soup at around two o'clock would suffice, with a large dinner to look forward to later.

Rose stretched her arm across Oliver's side of the bed. There was a rumpled dip where he'd been lying. It was still comfortingly warm. She immediately felt reassured but just wished she'd slept better. She still experienced a slight uneasiness, which was ridiculous bearing in mind the outcome of the investigation up the hill. What's more, there must be dozens of men with coats sporting similar style buttons to the one that she had picked up out of the snow and to the one worn by the man in the hotel last night. It was typical of the older generation's mountain dress, which they kept forever. In the cool, sensible light of a new day, everything seemed perfectly normal once more. Her body felt sated. Olly had remained full of gusto when they went to bed. It must have been that last drink at the bar which had pepped him up, even when he was so tired. She really did love him very much. She'd had two unsatisfactory love affairs when she was much younger; then, at twenty-six, Rose had met Olly and known, instantly, that he was the one she'd been waiting for: they'd been an item ever since. He was her soulmate. 'Well let's just hope that it lasts for ever. I never want to be alone again,' she thought, as smiling and with grey eyes twinkling he walked towards her from the bathroom. Rose would treat today as the real beginning of their holiday.

After a late lazy breakfast Oliver and Rose collected their equipment from the shop in the village, where the skis had been checked and fitted to their boots. Then they took the lift to the top of the mountain. Both sat quiet in the bubble as it slowly and steadily swung its way upward. The only noise was from the continuous gentle whir of the well-maintained machinery and the occasional call from the few colourful skiers far below. Almost like being in a cocoon, somewhere out of the real world and safe from harm, thought Rose: oddly she'd never before thought of it quite like that. But some people would understandably be terrified of these intricate pieces of machinery swinging them along from a great height. The trees were covered in a thick heavy blanket of new snow which glistened bewitchingly in the sunlight.

Oliver looked down on the slopes and thought that nothing had ever looked quite so inviting. He turned to Rose who, for the moment, was uncharacteristically deep in thought. Sitting beside him in her black padded jacket and scarlet ski pants, she looked every inch the capable skier that he knew her to be. Few men could keep up with her and even fewer women. Rose had spent a period at Grenoble University after leaving school, supposedly to learn French but, much to the annoyance of her father, had returned a competent skier, with only a mere smattering of the language she'd been sent there to learn. No matter now. Rose was well able to hold her own in conversation on their frequent visits to France. She was quick to learn when she put her mind to it.

Here the local people mostly spoke German, but many had a good understanding of both French and English. Oliver had also learnt to ski in the French Alps while on school holiday trips where he too had studied the language.

"A penny for them?" said Oliver, patting Rose on the knee and watching her face change as she returned, from wherever she'd been, to the present. Rose shrugged her shoulders and smiled a little self consciously.

"Oh dear...! sorry Olly, I was a million miles away, wasn't I? Actually, I was really just thinking how very beautiful it all is up here and how lucky we are as well."

"Yes, we are lucky, very lucky, but you're not still worrying about that business of the blood on the path are you?"

"Good heavens no," lied Rose, "of course not. That's all gone onto the back burner," at least for now, she added silently to herself. She leant against Oliver and kissed his cheek, her face alight with good humour once more.

They spent all afternoon skiing from one valley into the next, covering many miles; with so much of the powder snow as yet unspoilt, the conditions were perfect. Oliver and Rose were both capable and sensible as to where they skied and well aware of where the avalanche risks lay. Even so, very few people had either been their way before them, or dared to follow in their expert tracks. In this resort, off piste skiers were frowned upon unless judged to have the ability to extract themselves from trouble.

At the end of the day, before their final run down the mountain, Oliver and Rose stopped for a hot drink at a little hut well known to them on the edge of a forest. Few frequented this particular place of rest for it was truly remote. So they were surprised to see two pairs of skis propped outside the entrance.

The heat from the open fire hit them both in the face as they went in through the door. This was almost the best part of the day, thought Rose, pulling off her gloves and looking forward to a rest. Her fingers and toes were already beginning to tingle, now that they'd come in from the cold. Two men were sitting at the bar, talking to the man serving them. Both turned around together to inspect the newcomers.

"Hello," said Guy in pleased surprise.

"Hello," echoed his friend.

"Well hello, you two!" answered Oliver and Rose in unison.

Their two fellow hotel guests were drinking glühwein. Rose and Oliver happily agreed to join them.

"So, where are the girls?" Rose asked genuinely interested, as after last night she would have liked to have had the opportunity to get to know them both better.

"They went down for a massage a bit earlier," replied Guy, his eyes shining with merriment while he openly studied the attractive young woman standing before him. Rose in turn stared back, appraising his strong, fit-looking physique and noticing the slight but distinct Irish accent which was part of his charm.

"We have been given our orders not to have too many of these either, before coming down the mountain," added the other tall, fair man named Julian indicating his own almost empty glass as he got up to properly introduce himself.

"Well, I should imagine that it could prove a little difficult to negotiate the horrid narrow track from here and on down through the wood with too much of that on board," giggled Rose, privately agreeing with the advice of her absent new friends. Otto, the barman, chortled with mirth and in broken English asked the newcomers what they would like to help them on their way.

The four young people sat by the log fire, relaxed and comfortable in each other's company as they drank the strong and reviving mulled wine. Rose sat quietly, listening to the men prattling on about who'd skied which black run and when. She contemplated how easy they already were with each other. Then the subject changed and they got on to military tactics in troubled Middle Eastern countries. Judging by their well informed knowledge, Rose surmised that Julian and Guy had been in the Army together at some time and were obviously very old friends. They were a nice crowd and she was looking forward to seeing the girls again; perhaps they could all have dinner together. She might suggest it.

Rose didn't really relish a discussion about revolution and war at the moment. It really sounded too intense. She took another sip of her drink and felt the warm intoxicating liquid trickle slowly down her throat. The glowing embers of the fire were hot and would heighten the colour of her face. She didn't care; it was a good feeling, she'd taken a lot of exercise and in the cosy atmosphere she soon began to feel quite sleepy. She awoke with a start. The men were now talking about horrific earthquakes and tsunamis, how the world weather pattern was changing rapidly and that mankind, in many ways, should be held responsible; definitely time to interrupt.

"Oh my God, did I go to sleep?" she asked, rather embarrassed. Julian and Guy were watching her, amused. Oliver chuckled and leant across to gently touch her cheek.

"Yes, you did my darling. No matter, that's what a holiday is all about. But it's time to get you back now, for a hot bath; the light's beginning to fade and it will soon get very icy out there. Besides, Otto here will be wanting to pack up, go home and put his feet up." Otto merely smiled, genuinely pleased to have had the company in this very secluded place, which drew only the very best skiers.

Julian and Oliver went first, followed by Rose, with Guy bringing up the rear. It was icy, nastily so, and inside the wood it was also quite dark: they'd left it a bit late and so had to choose their way carefully. They were almost out of the wood when, on the last bend, Rose hit something hidden from sight; a ski came off and she went flying but landed safely, in a flurry of snow, beside the path. Guy was there in a flash.

"Are you alright?" he asked in a concerned voice, drawing up beside her with a well practiced flourish and stretching out an arm to help her up. "Lucky you didn't hit a tree."

"Yes I'm fine, don't worry," Rose replied laughing, getting up easily and brushing herself down. "First blood to me then: I'll bet neither of you have fallen yet!"

"No, but we haven't been here long, plenty of time to go! And you are an accomplished skier… you must have hit something: you're sure you are not hurt?" Rose nodded in answer. Guy took off his skis. "Okay stay there then, I'll go back for your lost transport!"

Guy retrieved her ski and found what she'd run into. He arrived back at her side, holding up the offending article for her to see.

"Look! This was your undoing. It's a dirty old coat, probably belonging to a woodsman," he laughed. "I should think he's missing it too, it's cold out…" He stopped abruptly, gaping at Rose's pale, shocked-looking face. She put out her hand to take the frozen garment from him.

"Rose... what is it? What on earth is the matter? You look like you have seen a ghost!"

"I think that perhaps I just have," she replied in a small, upset, voice holding the distasteful object up to inspect.

The piece of clothing wasn't particularly old and it hadn't been there for long. It was a grey duffle coat. Shaking off the snow, Rose could see that it had many blood stains and was missing a button which had been forcefully torn off.

She wouldn't say any more, but flung the coat away into the undergrowth of the forest. Rose then set off once more at speed to join the others who were waiting, worriedly, on the slope just outside the wood. There the run rejoined the piste down to the bottom of the mountain.

Guy also had seen the blood stains. He waited a moment to see Rose safely continue on her way to meet the others, then nipped back to have another look at the coat, afterwards replacing it under a log, out of sight. It took only a couple of minutes before he was slipping on his own skis again and following Rose on and out of the now grim, dark, forest.

"What happened?" called Oliver as they approached.

"It was nothing, nothing," replied Rose, sweeping on by without stopping. "I just fell on the ice Olly, that's all and I'm not hurt either, so forget it," she called back over her shoulder.

Oliver glanced at the Irishman as he sped past: Guy's face was difficult to read. He shrugged then raised his hands, letting his poles hang loosely; merely indicating that something untoward had just occurred but that perhaps it wasn't his for the telling. Julian and Oliver looked at each other, bewildered.

Oliver caught up with Rose and they skied down the gentle lower slopes together.

"What happened my darling? Did you crash? I was worried."

"No, not now Olly: I'll tell you when we get back." Her face had a set, determined look, but it didn't disguise the shock she'd quite obviously just suffered.

*

Rose was in a state. Oliver knew this because she'd hardly spoken since the fall and normally the only time she didn't speak was when she was upset, which wasn't often. He ran her a bath, squeezing a liberal amount of fragrant gel under the taps. Rose loved her bubbles. Making sure the temperature was just right, he picked her up from where she was sitting, shivering and naked, then unceremoniously plonked her in: a small smile returned to her face. This was promising, considered Oliver. He was on the right track.

"Now..." Olly pronounced firmly, "while I wash your back you can tell me what happened up there in the forest."

* * *

CHAPTER 4

"WHAT exactly took place up there in the wood?" asked the mystified Julian.

Rose and Oliver had gone up for a bath leaving the two men alone together in the little room off the bar, delaying the return to their rooms and the girls until they'd had a chance to discuss matters.

Guy recounted the incident just as it had happened on the way down through the forest.

"Rose is a brilliant skier, we weren't going fast and I couldn't understand why she'd fallen. Besides which, if there was something dangerous sticking up or concealed beneath the snow, I thought I'd better find it before someone else also came to grief."

"What was it then? What did you find?" interrupted Julian impatiently.

"A coat, covered in blood and... quite recently I'd say too, as the colour had hardly faded." He waited for the reaction. After a long pause Julian asked.

"Do you think the coat had merely been discarded after some unforeseen accident or... hidden on purpose? What sort of coat was it... a ski jacket?"

"No," responded Guy, "it was a duffle coat and it had been bundled up and half stuffed into a hole under the root of a tree: definitely not meant to be seen, in my opinion. Rose obviously just caught the edge of it, where she'd swerved trying to avoid a patch of black ice."

"Right, so we do have some mystery here," concluded Julian, "but we are bloody well supposed to be on holiday; do we really need to find out and become further involved?"

"I'm not sure yet, but I vote we go up and see our old friend Zak sometime tomorrow. We need to see him anyway: he'll know if there's anything going on that we need to worry about. Just don't say anything to the girls as yet, although I think I'll have to have a quiet word with Oliver."

"Yes, good idea... I like him, I like them both actually and I don't think he's the easily upset type either, do you?"

"No, not at all and it won't be difficult as we're all having dinner together tonight. We can stay later in the bar, after the girls go up to bed or something; anyway, I'll tip Oliver the wink beforehand. Now that's sorted I'm off to see if my lovely wife is hogging the bath."

"Good plan," agreed Julian getting up, "I'll follow suit, but I really do hope that our time here remains, as it should be... a proper uninterrupted and much needed break," he added morosely, remembering just how much the four friends had been looking forward to this time together.

*

Oliver was in a quandary. Should he now tell Rose about the disappearance of the man on the train? She'd be seriously fussed if he did. On the other hand, there was definitely something peculiar going on. The coincidences were becoming too many. Then he decided his course of action. The two other men he'd met seemed sensible down to earth people; he liked them a lot and the best plan might be to get them alone. It would be interesting to hear what they thought about it all. This plan of action made Oliver feel much better. He'd calmed Rose down by promising that he'd look into the 'blood in the snow' business in the morning and now she was looking forward to dinner with the others, as was he.

Rose was feeling calmer, but she remained absolutely certain that some crime had been committed further up the mountain and if Olly didn't do something about it, then she would. As a start, at the very first opportunity, she was going to speak to Hélène again and see if she really hadn't heard anything. She was very much looking forward to dinner with the other four, all of whom she felt to be kindred spirits. She was sure that the two men were thinking her a wimp for the upset, so Rose intended to choose her clothes carefully tonight and 'knock them all dead', Olly included! She sent him down to the bar first, reassuring him that she wouldn't be long in following.

Likewise, after their relaxing massages, both Alicia and Adriana also were slow in dressing. Consequently the three men found themselves together again, in the room off the bar, while they waited for the women to join them. It was a golden opportunity for a serious discussion.

✳

"That was really good fun," announced Rose when, sometime later, after having said goodnight to the others, she and Oliver went upstairs to their bedroom.

"But Olly are you sure you really want to go to the glacier tomorrow and ski all those foul black runs with Julian and Guy?"

"Yes, I would like to actually," answered Oliver, adding quickly "and it is only for one day. I thought you'd probably enjoy a lie-in, followed by a late breakfast, which Alicia and Adriana have already planned."

"No it's fine by me, but Olly you did promise…" She hesitated as he unlocked the door. Oliver put the key down on the side table and turned to Rose; her face showed a fleeting glimpse of anxious uncertainty. He came to her and put his arms around her protectively.

"I know what I said my darling. I will look into that business up the mountain and if there has been a crime committed I guarantee that I shall find out about it, so you mustn't fuss. Alright?" Rose was relieved and, with a bright smile, began to get undressed.

"Here," said Olly grabbing her by the belt, "let me help you!"

❄

The three men left at first light, long before the ski stations were even open. Together, in snow boots, they trudged up the road. The pre-arranged snowmobiles were waiting, under covers behind a log hut just below the middle station. Guy automatically took command, just as he always had in the past, Julian thought wryly.

"Oliver, will you come behind me please?" He handed his back pack to Julian and threw his leg across the machine. Oliver took his place on the leather-covered seat, at the back. He was correct in his assumption after their short meeting in the bar last night just before dinner: these two men were not only dead cool, but also extremely good at organising unusual transport at the drop of a hat. They had definitely been involved in this sort of adventure before. Oliver was looking forward to being further enlightened.

The machines started at once and they moved off up the un-pisted track, one behind the other. The snow was thick on the ground and it satisfactorily muffled the noise of their progress. The trees on either side were heavily weighted. Birds were now stirring, creating soft flurries of snow as they flew disturbed from the upper branches. The sun was as yet nothing more than a pale pink glimmer of promise behind the mountain top above them. Oliver found himself thoroughly enjoying this unexpected and rather clandestine journey. Rose would have a fit if she knew what they were really about.

Julian was having trouble coming to terms with the realization that their holiday had been so rudely interrupted. He would very much prefer to have been cosily tucked up beside his sleeping girlfriend. Adriana also was oblivious as to what the men were doing.

Guy, on the other hand, had no trouble whatsoever slotting back into secret service work-mode. He felt the adrenalin flow through his body and realized just how much he revelled in this kind of mission. His everyday work at home was tame by comparison. Alicia was the only one of the three girls who had cottoned on to this particular enigmatic plan. As they progressed up the mountain, Guy chuckled silently to himself, remembering their earlier exchange as he'd tip-toed out of the bathroom to get dressed: he'd heard her gentle, sleepy voice.

"You're not going skiing this morning, are you my darling?" She had laughed softly at his sharp intake of breath then, "I'm not stupid you know. I'm well aware that you're up to something else and that it has something to do with Rose's fall. However, I'm sure you'll tell me when you're ready... just be careful that's all..." and she turned over to go to sleep again.

Guy had merely sighed, smiled to himself in the dark and bent to kiss his wife before leaving.

Ten minutes later they were on the path where Rose had fallen. Guy knew exactly where he had hidden the coat and had no trouble retrieving it. All three men stood together, the sudden silence somewhat eerie in the half light as they inspected the coat with a torch. Oliver produced the button that Rose had found by the blood. It matched those on the coat of course, just as he'd known it would. Guy removed a large plastic bag from his pocket and shaking the coat free of snow carefully rolled it up, placed it in the protective bag and stowed it away into the back pack.

"Well, there's no doubt about that then," affirmed Guy. "Let's now go on up and see if our friend Zak can throw any light on the matter."

"Where are we going to now?" asked Oliver, trying to contain his growing excitement.

"We are going on a magical mystery tour, further up the mountain and up with the eagles," answered Guy with a wink at Julian.

Oliver watched in fascination: Julian took an odd looking brush affair from the storage compartment of each snowmobile and fixed it securely to the back of each machine. Once the others were aboard facing up hill and ready to go, Julian restarted his own vehicle then drove it back and forth where they had all been standing. Soon every trace of their prints had been completely wiped out and the way neatly pisted. Oliver, sitting behind Guy, thought that this particular day was becoming more interesting by the minute.

They journeyed on up to the crest of the mountain range, well above the highest ski lift, to where a narrow pass took them into another hidden valley. The rising sun now hit them full in the face, blinding them with all its force. Guy slowed down, then suddenly dived off the path and through the dark entrance to a cave. He cut the engine and dismounted. Julian, following close behind, did likewise. Guy turned to address the astonished Oliver.

"As you have probably realized we don't feel it necessary to advertise our presence on this particular part of the mountain. We are here for a purpose and I have to ask, before we go any further, that from now on you keep everything you see or hear to yourself. Not even Rose must know anything of our movements. As far as the girls are concerned we have gone skiing, on the glacier, as was planned." Oliver nodded.

"I quite understand: I knew just from the little time that we spent alone together last night that, in the past, you two must have had dealings with the undercover world, but where are we going to now?" he asked once more.

"We are going to meet an old friend with whom we have worked on various occasions. He has a 'hidey-hole' up here and is sure to know of anything untoward presently taking place in this area. He knows we are coming but not exactly when. So, just for the hell of it, we are going to see how near to the safe house we can get before he actually spots us." Julian was now grinning and with a certain relish added:

"It's good practice, like a sort of exercise; we always do it."

"So far," continued Guy, "we have never quite got all the way. This fact makes Zak very proud and one day we have to reverse that situation. It could be today if we are lucky and keep our wits about us." He laughed. "OK now let's get dressed up."

Oliver was given snow shoes, two expanding sticks and a hooded camouflage-coloured suit, which were identical to those the other two had on. He was thoroughly enjoying himself.

They set off in single file along the tree line on a much used animal track. To the right was a sheer drop directly above the ski area. Oliver could just see the highest lifts over the edge. To the left was a steeply wooded mountain incline below which he couldn't see. The men made slow progress as in places the snow had drifted into such huge mounds that they had to skirt their way around. Oliver had just decided that he was getting the hang of the snow shoes when Guy suddenly stopped and took his off, strapping them to his back.

"Now I'm afraid we have the difficult bit," he turned to Oliver. "Count to ten then follow me. Just copy whatever I do. We are going down."

"Going down... down where for God's sake?" Oliver spluttered. "There is no way down!"

"Oh yes there is, you'll see." With that Guy stepped left, dropped to his knees, curled into a ball and started to slide down between the trees. Julian was chuckling as he made Olly also remove his special winter footwear which he then shook free of snow and secured to the strap across Oliver's back.

"It's too steep to get down any other way. OK," he said playfully thumping Olly on the shoulder. "Your turn. Off you go then, just keep in Guy's path, roll up the same and you'll be fine. I'll be right behind you."

Oliver decided that the only thing to do was to go quickly, without hesitation; this was similar to the Outward Bound Territorial Army course he'd completed after leaving school. He knew how to coil and tense his body, balance his weight and protect his head with his arms. Guy was now at the bottom of the slope, standing up, brushing himself down and waiting for the others to arrive. Olly bombed down even faster and landed in a flurry at Guy's feet, closely followed by Julian. Bent almost double, the three men then moved carefully through the trees to the edge of the wood, where they crouched, looking out. Before them lay a seemingly unspoilt secret valley; at first Oliver couldn't see a dwelling of any sort. They stayed still, watching for any sign of life while considering how to negotiate the open space in front of them: just a short distance to traverse but with no cover whatsoever.

"There's only one way across this bit," Oliver was scrutinizing a snow laden copse in the middle of the open valley; the trees, touched by the early morning sun, had caught his attention: that must be their goal. He thought he could just detect a trail of smoke, perhaps from a chimney; yes, he could smell it. Their destination must be there, hidden amongst the trees.

"How's that then?" asked Guy, amused.

"On our stomachs," replied Olly briskly shading his eyes against the glare.

"Quite right too," answered Guy, impressed. "But there is another way, although it would take longer. We could keep to the trees and move around in a semi circle, to come in from the north, where there is a shorter distance to crawl. What do you think Julian?"

"It'll take much too long in this snow and, more importantly, we'd disturb the wildlife which in turn would announce our presence," interrupted Oliver, getting thoroughly into the whole business. "Also..." he added, "the depth of snow alone will actually give us plenty of cover." Julian looked at Guy and raised his eyebrows in surprise.

"He's good," remarked Julian, "very good indeed. Maybe he's in the wrong job!"

Guy nodded in agreement, grinning, then returned to the task in hand.

"Now let's see how far we can get before Zak discovers us. We can leave the back packs here beneath this undergrowth and pick them up later. I'll go first, Oliver will you please follow me again?"

✳ ✳ ✳

CHAPTER 5

ROSE was the last into the dining room, rushing in just before breakfast ended.

"I am so sorry," she said to the others, "I went back to bed after Olly left and just overslept."

"Couldn't matter less," replied Alicia, "we would have kept you some food anyway." Adriana moved up and patted the seat beside her. "Come on, sit down. We are very relaxed skiers when we are on our own and, without the bossy ones giving us orders, there's no hurry at all, really there isn't."

Rose sat down, relieved. They ordered fresh coffee. Hélène brought it over with two extra cups.

"Hello Rose, *Guten Morgen*, I'm helping out with breakfast this morning, as some of the staff have gone off for a meeting with my husband. It's quiet for the moment so perhaps I can sit with you all for a minute.

"Please do!" the three girls chorused, moving up on the banquette seating to make more space. Rose went to collect some food from the buffet and came back munching happily on a croissant. She listened as the other two tried to persuade the discreet Hélène to tell them the latest gossip about some of their more intriguing guests.

"And what about the delectable doctor you told us about, Hélène. Has he arrived yet?" asked Adriana, with undisguised interest. Then, on noting her friend's face, adding somewhat sheepishly, "Don't look at me like that Ally. I'm still single: at least for the moment I seem to be."

Alicia laughed a little sympathetically.

"Well, only sort of single; depends how you look at it really. Anyway that's all going to change for certain this holiday! You'll see." Adriana merely smiled an 'I wish' back at her.

"Don't worry," replied Hélène picking up on the light-hearted banter. "You've missed the taxi. The doctor is already spoken for. I'll introduce you in a minute. He's just gone up to his room. His train was late but he said he'd be down for a cup of coffee shortly, before going out to get his skis. He's charming and so is his other half although she can't get away until the end of the week, unfortunately: you'll like them both, I'm sure. And why are you all laughing? Did I say something wrong?"

"No, I'm afraid that we are being really mean and teasing you, Hélène," replied Alicia smiling. "It's just that you miss the 'bus', not the 'taxi'."

"Well, what's the difference, the meaning is the same?" replied Hélène laughing good-naturedly.

"Exactly, but don't ever change, Hélène, because your English is absolutely charming and we all love it."

"Thank you," answered Hélène accepting the upside down compliment. She was very fond of these people; they were both genuine and good company and she always looked forward to their visits.

Rose had just finished eating when the doctor put in his expected appearance. He came over to their table, positively beaming in recognition, his face alight with pleasure. Alicia and Adriana let out shrieks of delight as soon as they saw him, for they'd all met before. Hélène introduced him to Rose and, grinning happily, the new arrival was easily persuaded to sit down with them all at the table.

Marc had dark, curly auburn-coloured hair, a face that often saw the sun and brown-flecked, twinkling eyes. Rose immediately took to him. He looked intelligent and capable, but also fun, she thought studying him as he talked. She sensed a kind and deeply sensitive man; somebody you could rely on. Adriana wished he could have been her doctor and as before, when they'd first met, decided she wouldn't have minded being ill, just once in a while, in order to receive his ministrations.

Hélène and Rose sat listening as Alicia explained and described where they had all met two years before at a barbeque on a little island in the Ionian sea off mainland Greece. Obviously it had been an exceptionally special time, particularly as they had all returned to celebrate Marc and Emma's wedding in the autumn. He had family living there so often visited the island, a second home to him.

"But where is Emma?" asked Adriana, butting in, burning with curiosity. "Why isn't she here?" Alicia, just in case there was a problem, kicked her friend hard under the table. Marc, noticing, smiled full of good humour.

"Everything's fine, Emma's coming, but not until the end of the week. She was furious to be left behind, but someone in the office let her down. She couldn't get enough help to run the travel agency. So, with much deliberation, it was decided that I should come ahead, as planned, direct from the USA. It seemed silly to waste both tickets just for two days but," he added rather sadly, "I have to admit I didn't really want to arrive here, in this lovely place, without her."

"But surely you will still have plenty of time together, won't you?" asked Rose conscious of his dejected expression.

"Oh yes." Marc's face brightened. "We will have ten whole days together and actually, having just flown in

47

from America, I'm quite pleased to have a few days' peace to recover before Emma gets here."

"Brilliant," pronounced Adriana, "Guy and Julian will be so thrilled to see you. I can't wait for them to get back from the glacier and, at the end of the week, for us all to be complete."

❄

"I'm sorry your train was so late; that's very unusual," apologised Hélène, when she could get in a word. She was concerned as always for her guests' welfare. "I wonder what the reason was?"

"Yes well, actually, there was rather an unusual occurrence." The young doctor's face clouded and he hesitated. "I hate to be the bringer of bad tidings, but I suppose it was rather lucky that I was on that particular train, as there was a rather nasty drama I had to deal with." Rose sat bolt upright: her eyes startled.

"What drama? What happened on the train? Please tell us." Marc noticed the keen interest and the worried expression, almost as if the pretty, dark girl anticipated what he was about to say. He turned towards her and as diplomatically as possible, leaving out the gory details, recounted his earlier experience on the train.

"There was a body by the line. A suicide they think, not a local person, but from foreign parts I gather," he hastily reassured Hélène placing his hand on her arm. "Anyway, as a doctor, I was called upon to make sure that the man was well and truly dead, before the train could continue on its journey."

The girls sat dumbstruck, staring at Marc as they digested what he'd just said.

Rose's face was the colour of parchment. Marc looked at the four attractive women sitting around the table. They were all speechless and understandably horrified.

"Well, I'm sorry; not a very nice way to begin your day, but I'm afraid you were bound to hear of it sooner or later," he said, trying to cheer them up a bit.

"A body!" exclaimed Alicia. "A suicide! Here?"

"Somebody dead, I can't believe it!" blustered Adriana.

"Good heavens!" was all that Hélène could manage. The dead silence continued while they all digested this extraordinary piece of news.

"Where exactly did this happen?" Finally, Rose's small voice broke the charged quietness.

"Just outside the village," the doctor replied, turning to their hostess and suggesting quickly, "Hélène how about some jägertee instead of the coffee? I know I could do with something a bit stronger myself," he checked his watch, "and actually it's still night-time for me!"

"Yes, a good idea; poor Marc you really have had a rotten start to your day. You must be exhausted having just flown in from America and with all this horrible business to help investigate." Hélène got up, removed the half finished cups, placed them on the nearby tray and hurried off. Rose was sitting still, looking particularly stunned. Marc turned towards her once more.

"Come on Rose; these things do happen you know, although I'm sure it is extremely unusual up here in these mountains." He touched her shoulder encouragingly. She noticed that he appeared really concerned for her and she liked him, so she was going to inquire: she had to know.

"Could I just ask you something please… the dead man…" then it came out in a rush, "he wasn't wearing a coat, was he?"

Her eyes were wide and frightened-looking. Rose vaguely heard one of the others mutter something, gasp and call her name but she couldn't concentrate on anybody else except the doctor. She could hear her own heart beating, her hands were beginning to sweat and she felt both hot and cold as she waited for his answer. The seconds ticked by, nobody spoke and everybody stared at Marc. He thought for a minute. What a strange question. Then, he remembered.

"No, oddly enough, you are right. The dead man wasn't wearing a coat, but how on earth did you…?" Rose uttered a small, animal-like whimper, shot up and squeezed her way out from behind the table and past the others, mumbling excuses, then rushed across the room towards the ladies room.

"What on earth is going on here?" Marc inquired breaking the silence and now totally in professional mode. His own brow was furrowed in puzzlement as he looked at the other astonished faces around him. Alicia jumped up, "God knows! Well… I'd better go and see if Rose is alright."

Hélène also was stunned by the news of a violent death so near her hotel, which was normally a haven of peace and tranquillity. But when she returned with the hot drinks she endeavoured to be calmly reassuring.

"I think I will just go to find Anton and get him to check all this out with the police. Please excuse me, but let me know if you need anything for Rose; I hope she's alright," she added, glancing doubtfully towards the wash rooms, before hurrying away again. Adriana and Marc were left at the table. She was the first to speak.

"Rose knows something about this incident, or thinks she does."

"Yes, but what could she possibly know about it? The man was a foreigner and, judging from his appearance, had been dead for sometime. He was in a bad state, but without a post-mortem it's hard to tell what actually killed him, especially in this ultra cold climate. I was only asked to confirm that the poor chap was dead. The rest will come later and will be dealt with locally. My train was the first up this morning and I suppose, in the dark, the body would have gone unnoticed, otherwise he would have been found earlier. As it was the poor man was half frozen. But I can't imagine what it could possibly have to do with Rose, can you?"

Before Adriana could answer, Alicia and Rose came out of the wash room together. Rose was feeling better. Alicia believed what she had to say and also had a suggested plan of action. The staff were returning from their meeting with Anton and beginning to prepare the tables for lunch. Alicia realized that they would be overheard.

"I suggest we move elsewhere and hear what Rose has to tell us. Marc, I'm sorry, I know that you have only just got here and you must be out on your feet, but I think that we do need your expertise on this one."

"Of course, it's no problem the jägertee has done the trick. I feel decidedly rejuvenated! We'll go to the little room off the bar; there's not likely to be anybody there at this time of day. They may well have already lit the fire so it will be nice and cosy. Come Rose, don't worry we'll get to the bottom of it all." Rose looked at them all gratefully.

"Thanks; you have no idea just how good it will be to get all of this off my chest."

Guy was making for the last available bit of cover before crossing into the wood. They'd made good progress but needed a rest. Oliver must have been exhausted and yet hadn't held them up at all. When they achieved their goal, the patch of scrub, they were able to sit together and stretch their aching limbs. Julian, peering through the bushes, scanned the edge of the wood with his binoculars.

"Not a sign of movement yet," he was whispering, "this is the nearest we have ever got. If we can get unseen into the wood it'll be a first." Guy was in his element and full of enthusiasm.

"You're good on your stomach, Oliver. How come you're so fit?"

"I do regular stints with the TA and run every morning, before work," he replied, pleased with their obvious admiration.

"Um! Useful sort of bloke to have around," muttered Julian, still observing the wood.

"Any sign of the Alsatians?" Guy asked.

"No, and we are still well downwind."

Thank God for that, thought Oliver, determined not to let on that he was terrified of Alsatians. He had thus far entered into this whole adventure with a certain gusto, but at this point wondered if it might not be a good idea to make themselves known to the elusive Zak. He also hoped that there might be a warm fire and something to eat when they reached their destination: he was starving.

The three men crawled the last few yards, in a snake-like fashion, arriving at the edge of the wood where they found another resting place amidst a circular area of brush, well beaten down by some animal. Guy pulled himself into a sitting position, put his fingers to his lips, then indicated behind him smiling and nodding his head.

"Guten Morgen, Zak!"

There followed the noise of a human grunt, footsteps in the snow and the muffled whine of a dog: Zak appeared from behind the bushes. He was grinning like a Cheshire cat. The man was short dark and stocky and had a very sun-tanned face.

"Guten Tag to you all," he laughed, slapping the two friends on the back in greeting, then turning politely to shake Oliver by the hand.

"Once again you almost made it," he said chuckling, "but not quite; a little further perhaps this time, but not much! Never mind: it's my job to see you get no nearer and I have a very good reason at present. Come back to the house where I will explain and introduce you to my guest."

"Good," replied Guy, "I hoped you might have something for us."

"And I need a cigarette after leaving my bed so early on our supposed vacation," added Julian somewhat morosely, "so let's go." Zak let out another guffaw indicating his amusement.

"It's time you gave up smoking, Julian. Adriana hates it. I'm surprised you haven't made an honest woman of that beautiful girl yet. You should marry her quickly, before someone else comes along and snatches her away from under your nose," he teased, leaning towards his friend and colleague and tapping his own appendage delightedly.

"Yes, well; I'm thinking about it. But she, lucky thing, is all cosy and warm at the moment, enjoying a decent breakfast without me and I haven't had anything to eat since dinner last night."

"Don't worry. I'll look after you... haven't I always?" Zak, still full of good humour, set off with the dogs still firmly on their leads, much to Oliver's relief.

*

Marc listened with interest to everything that Rose had to say. There was no doubt about it: something extremely untoward was afoot. He leant forward, the others waiting attentively.

"I have a plan." Rose realized, thankfully, that Marc also believed her.

"I vote that we go up to this place on the track and see what else we can find." He looked at the three expectant faces.

"I think that's a brilliant idea," replied Alicia without hesitation. "Do you think we might be able to find some traces of the frozen blood, all covered over?"

"Yes, that could prove extremely useful, but I also need to retrieve the coat: we'll need a couple of spades, which we can borrow from the hotel, and some sort of container. I'll organize that, so why don't you all go and get togged up and we'll meet in the reception area in about twenty minutes, if that suits? But not a word to anybody: at least for the moment. I'll say that we need the shovels for helping dig out a car and the plastic box for biscuits to keep us going until our next meal."

Adriana and Rose jumped up and headed for the stairs which led to their rooms. Marc called after them,

"Rose, can you bring that button with you please?"

"Yes, of course." She answered waving as she followed Adriana upstairs. Alicia hesitated until the others were out of earshot.

"I presume," she said, turning to Marc "that you're thinking that there could, just possibly, be a DNA match between the dead man by the railway line, the frozen blood up the mountain and even on the coat?"

"Yes, I do think it's quite possible and then the suicide notion would become extremely suspect."

"Well, I think that perhaps we should call in the cavalry, when they get back from skiing, as they do have some experience in these matters. Actually, I think it's quite likely that they are already aware that our idyllic mountains may not be quite as tranquil as usual."

Marc turned to look directly into Alicia's clear, bright blue eyes.

"Good... let's get ready and then go on up and see what we can find. Perhaps this evening we can pool our resources. I'm looking forward to seeing the others again. What a great surprise to find you all here. Emma will be thrilled."

※ ※ ※

CHAPTER 6

ROSE was ready and waiting at the bottom of the stairs and appeared quite agitated when the other two girls came down a few minutes later.

"What's the matter Rose?" asked Adriana, noticing immediately and indicating that they should all walk out of earshot, away from the reception desk.

"It's the button, it's gone," she answered in a rush. "I put it away really carefully. No-one would have known where to find it..." she hesitated putting her hands to either side of her face thinking, then looking startled as an idea dawned, "except for Olly of course, but surely he wouldn't have taken it. Why would he?" Adriana glanced at Alicia who was about to reply when they were all distracted by a waft of cold air as some people came in from outside; so they moved back into the warmth of the sitting room behind the bar.

Marc followed some newly arrived guests through the hotel entrance, politely helping them in with their luggage and quickly closing the door behind them. It was minus seven out there – cold. He'd checked the thermometer which hung on a hook by the ski rack. The girls were nowhere to be seen but he could hear muffled voices coming from the direction of the bar; they were there standing in a little huddle, talking animatedly. He went to join them guessing something more was amiss.

"What ever has happened in... let me see..." he glanced at his watch, "in just less than twenty minutes? I thought you might all be late," he added as a rather male chauvinist aside trying to lighten the mood. As soon as he'd said it he realized it was a mistake. Damn! Alicia turned towards him. Her beautiful blue eyes regarded him coolly in the face of his intended jollity.

"The button has gone and, apart from Rose, there is only one other person who knew where it was and that's Oliver but..." she continued with a certain relish and a quick smile, "I think I know why it's gone." The others all gaped at her.

"Why... where is it? Who has taken it? How could you possibly know?" asked a tremulous Rose. Adriana was smiling at her friend, understanding and waiting for Alicia to explain further.

"Well," said Alicia to her rapt audience, "it's just that I don't believe our men have gone skiing on the glacier at all: I think they are up to something else altogether." She glanced at the astonished Rose and put a reassuring hand on her arm.

"Fear not Rose the cavalry are already on the case. Dr Watson here has his kit, so let's go and I'll explain as much as I can on the way up the mountain."

Marc, grinning good-naturedly and accepting Alicia's slight rebuff, began to usher them all out of the door. Both blonde women were obviously concerned for Rose and he quite understood their feelings. The young waitress rearranging the bar stools was looking curious, she must have already heard something about the dead man. He'd also have to talk to Hélène later to reassure her, with some justification, about Rose's odd behaviour at breakfast. Meanwhile it certainly was time to make a move. It would be good for everybody to take some action and to get out into the fresh air.

The doctor had managed to borrow two snow shovels from the odd-job man and a plastic picnic box, together with a spoon, from the kitchen. It had been difficult explaining to the hospitable kitchen staff that he actually wanted the container empty. They were used to making up lunch boxes for cross country skiers. When the girls were ready they gathered up the equipment and set off up the hill to the bend in the road, where the track began.

By the time the small group arrived at the appointed place, Rose and Marc were aware that both Julian and Guy had a mysterious past. Although Alicia was only able to divulge certain aspects, it was still enough to inspire confidence in the others. In their separate, clandestine 'other' world, her husband Guy and his old schoolmate Julian were extremely experienced professionals.

Rose directed her new friends to the spot where she'd first come across the blood. Marc went to look under the bushes, as Oliver had done two days before. The ugly trap and faint, acrid animal smell remained, but the marmot, its life's blood having ebbed away into the disturbed dried leaves and earth beneath, had been spirited away: poor thing. There were several footprints around and about, giving some credence to Rose's disturbing story, and the snow had been piled high beside the trail. They worked for half an hour, carefully taking it in turns to dig and search the snow on either side of the little footway. There was no sign of anything untoward. Rose dug furiously until her arms ached and she was hot and pink in the face. She was determined not to have to admit defeat. Alicia, watching, came across to take her turn with the spade. Rose handed it over somewhat begrudgingly then, throwing up her hands in a helpless gesture of despair, walked away to hide her disappointment, while the others worked on.

She was following a vague track, leading off at right angles, lower down the path when Rose noticed further traces of half-covered footprints. It looked as if a small vehicle of some sort had passed this way, probably the small piste basher responsible for the clearance. She looked up ahead, trying to see where the marks went, but they seemed to peter out. There was nothing, only another heap of snow. Rose kicked at the soft mound in frustration and her foot hit something hard, a tree stump or stick perhaps: letting out a yelp, she bent to brush the snow off the offending object and there before her lay what appeared to be the much sought after evidence for which they were all searching. The frozen blood: dirty-looking now, admittedly, but the colour was still quite unmistakeable, encased in misshapen, broken chunks of icy horror, all stuck together and contrasting starkly with the pure white of the new snow surrounding it. The reality that she'd found what she was looking for was something to contend with. Her shout had brought the others to her side and they found Rose staring, almost in disbelief, at her findings.

"It is the blood, isn't it?" she asked of Marc. "It's almost rust-coloured now."

"Yes, it certainly appears that you have hit the jackpot Rose, but let's just have a closer look." The girls leant over Marc's shoulder as he bent to examine the grim discovery. Rose held her breath, her heart thumping. Marc stood up, then rifled around in his pocket, taking out a small plastic scoop and the container.

"It's blood alright, although a little discoloured by the freezing temperatures. The cold has helped preserve it so there will be no trouble in testing to see if it's animal or human."

"Which do you think it is?" demanded Rose, desperate to have her story confirmed. Marc smiled at her understandable impatience.

"I really can't say for certain, not out here. But I do agree there seems to be an awful lot of it for a small animal or even a minor human accident. Anyway why bother to cover it up in such a hurry if it was just an accident? Hardly anybody uses this way down. I'll take it in right away, as I have to go and give a statement to the police this afternoon; I already have an appointment. Don't worry, we should know shortly. The Swiss are very efficient in these matters especially if there's the possibility of a crime." He began to hack at the frozen lump with a penknife then, most carefully, spooned horrid little ice cube sized pieces of the discoloured evidence into the box. The three girls watched as if mesmerized.

"Yuck," uttered Adriana. "Imagine: all that could have belonged inside a person. Would it be too gory a question to ask what sort of injury would have caused such a great loss of blood?"

"A severed main artery, most likely," answered Marc without preamble, straightening up and snapping shut the lid on the container. He glanced up at the sky. "There's more snow forecast later, but I think that we need to conceal our tracks a bit first, just in case a guilty someone comes back and finds their choice heap of snow disturbed."

They thoroughly covered over the evidence again and with a small branch swept away the tell tale footprints, both around the mound and leading back up to the main track, as they walked. Alicia, who had been deep in thought on the way back to the hotel, asked Marc the question which had been bothering her.

"As a doctor, wouldn't you have known if the dead man you examined by the railway line had had his throat cut, or whatever?"

"Yes and he hadn't had his throat cut. I could see that. But I'm afraid the poor chap was in such an awful state and the rest of his body so badly broken that, without a post-mortem, it was impossible to guage which injury had actually killed him. I wasn't allowed to move him and there could have been a lot more frozen blood underneath. The only thing that I could confirm was that he'd been dead for some hours; he was quite cold. Then the various authorities were called and we moved on. Also..." he turned to Rose, who was walking beside him, her hands thrust deep in her pockets, "I did think it odd, at the time, that the wretched man was coatless; which makes me think that he could easily have been tossed there, already dead, by the line, giving the appearance that he had been hit and flung aside by a train!"

"But if he was dumped," Adriana chipped in, "surely the person or people who deposited the body can't seriously have thought that a slow moving Swiss mountain train was a good enough candidate to be considered for a suicide scenario?"

"Ah!" interrupted Rose, "but how about if the dumpers were foreigners also, with not a clue about Swiss mountain trains? They might have thought that they rushed headlong through the night, mowing down everything in their way, cows included?"

"Good God!" Marc laughed. "Talk about conjecture! First of all let's wait and see who, or what, the blood belongs to."

On their return to the hotel the girls ordered hot drinks and Marc went upstairs to his room to deposit the plastic box safely in his mini fridge-freezer. It was then decided that the women would go skiing, as if nothing strange was afoot and, if they came down the forest track finally, they could collect the coat on passing. Marc, not wishing to leave the container unattended for long would try to advance his afternoon meeting with the police. They would assemble again, back in the hotel, after dark, when hopefully Guy, Julian and Oliver would have returned.

After lunch, when the three girls were in the ski lift bubble on their way up the mountain, Alicia, with an uneasy expression on her face, made a rather sobering announcement.

"A thought has just occurred to me." The others turned to look at her. "If a murder has indeed been committed on this mountain, by a person or persons as yet unknown, then for the moment and until our men return I think that we three had better stick closely together. If we were seen earlier collecting the evidence, we could all be in a slight predicament: Rose in particular, if she was seen finding it in the first place." They all sat silently contemplating this statement, then Rose replied in a small voice:

"Oh dear, yes I suppose you're right, I might have been observed snooping. It was quite early and the people responsible might not long have cleared the path. Although I didn't see a soul out there, I suppose someone could easily have been watching from the trees. Heavens what a scary thought. I'm so sorry, it's all my fault for finding the beastly blood in the first place... and we're all meant to be here relaxing. What about Marc?"

"He's in it as well now, though the sooner he gets that box with its horrible contents to the police the better," replied Adriana. "Anyway there's no point in worrying as, let's face it... it might not be human blood after all, which would mean that we are, unnecessarily, making a meal out of the whole thing."

"I bet it is," mumbled Rose getting off the lift and carrying her skis to a flat piece of ground where she could more easily put them on. She glanced around at their fellow skiers; perfectly normal looking young people enjoying themselves. The conditions were brilliant. She could be wrong and it was silly to be nervous. The others were ready and so she smiled at them encouragingly. It was time to be positive.

"I agree." Rose said sounding enthusiastic. "There's absolutely nothing to be done for the moment, let's get some exercise. Who's going first? Last to the middle station buys the first round of glühwein." Good humour once again restored, all three set off down the slope in a competent and conspicuous line of athletic excellence.

✳

At precisely three thirty that afternoon, down in the town of Spiegelsee, Marc left the Polizeiwache, having received the pathology results from the forensic department. His usually cheerful face carried an expression of extreme alarm. The situation regarding the suicide death on the line had changed dramatically. How could he have been so stupid; he should never have suggested the girls go skiing alone: there was a murderer at large.

✳　✳　✳

CHAPTER 7

FAR up the mountain in the hidden valley, inside the safe house, Oliver sat beside the wood-burning stove, his hands cradling a mug of laced tea; thawing out. He'd already wolfed down a beef sandwich and could have done with another but didn't like to ask. Zak, his considerate host, was now busy with more important matters. Olly had never enjoyed himself so much as he had this morning, in the company of these two extraordinary new friends of his: Guy Hargreaves and Julian Birchall. It was odd that their paths had never crossed before, as they were all frequent visitors to the Hotel Sonne und Schnee. He now understood that the men's regular jobs back in England were a mere front and that when on occasion they travelled on so called business, the 'business' was in reality a very different, secret type of work.

Oliver listened, fascinated, to the illuminating conversation between the two Englishmen and Zak. When he heard the words defection and escape enter the conversation, he soon realized that they were all in the middle of an international incident of mammoth proportions. He sat quietly and surreptitiously studied the foreign guest: the disappearing mystery man, who had been on the early morning train. When they'd politely shaken hands just now, the man had hardly acknowledged Oliver as someone he'd seen before. Olly now understood that the poor man had been too involved with his own precarious position to notice those around him on his journey up into these mountains. He felt sorry for him. Defection was a desperate measure. The man's last few days must have been nothing short of a nightmare. He must have had a dreadful dilemma whilst trying to keep his valuable knowledge intact. Do you leave your family, perhaps never to see them again, or do you stay in your politically unstable country where your expertise could be used to the detriment of world peace?

On closer inspection, the guest was a middle aged, nice looking man of Aryan extraction, sitting quietly in a corner, reading. Oliver remembered learning a little about Iran and its people. He'd like to follow the Persian 'silk route' with Rose one day. He knew the meaning of the word Aryan – noble; it somehow suited this man. He looked so sad, yet somewhat resigned to his fate. By his side, on the arm of his chair, lay another grey duffle coat, identical to the one that they'd brought up with them, except that theirs was covered in blood stains. How many grey duffle-coated men were there on this particular mountain? What about the exceptionally unfriendly individual he'd seen in the hotel; who was he? He wasn't at all like this polite, learned man presently here with them in the safe house. Guy came across to where Oliver was sitting and squatted down beside him.

"Oliver, you will have already heard a certain amount here this morning that you mustn't repeat, but I think it's best if I fill you in with the rest and then you will understand the predicament in which we find ourselves." Zak and Julian came to join them and perched on stools in front of the fire.

"So much for our carefree holiday," mumbled Julian getting out another cigarette. Guy took no notice. He was used to Julian occasionally lapsing into moroseness and so he carried on regardless.

"As no doubt you have gathered from what has been said so far, the man sitting in the corner behind me is a very eminent and distinguished Persian scientist. Don't worry, he can't keep up with what I am saying if I speak both quickly and quietly." Oliver again glanced across at the foreigner, but the man still seemed oblivious and lost in his book. He must be thoroughly traumatized thought Olly. Guy continued.

"His work in Iran is a nuclear project. You must know that Iran's government is made up of both elected and unelected institutions and some of these people genuinely believe that, by whatever means, they are destined to lead a fanatical war against their so-called Israeli enemies. It is thought that the Russians and the North Koreans have been instrumental in helping Iran develop its nuclear capability. The scientist, Ahmad, one of a key group, was unhappy with this work which was of obvious and incalculable world concern. After much soul searching he has fled his country and is seeking political asylum here. The others, including a Russian and a Pakistani scientist, elected to stay, in spite of another of their team being killed by a car bomb just a short while ago. You probably heard it on the news?" Oliver nodded and Guy carried on.

"Ahmad left his family behind hoping that once here, if he traded his vital knowledge, his wife and sons might manage to follow. In my opinion they are likely to be undergoing intensive interrogation as we speak and are probably at least under house arrest. They will be watched like hawks and helping them also to leave the country, at present, would be well nigh impossible. As it was our friend here had a great deal of trouble getting out. Iran, geographically, is like a fortress, hence all the problems for invading armies in ancient times. The borders are well manned and so it must have taken a lot of covert organization for his friends to arrange his departure. A prominent scientist such as he would have been conspicuous even in his own place of birth. Ahmad was an extremely valuable asset. He evidently couldn't leave in any normal way. He had never before been out of Iran and he couldn't ask for help outside his own country because Iran's present relationship with the rest of the world is extremely fragile. As you know there is no longer an Iranian Embassy in London. They are flexing their muscles by testing their missiles out at sea. Tension is growing worldwide. God alone knows what they are actually capable of now. On top of it all, on this occasion, our combined intelligence services had no prior knowledge of this man's intended defection.

"Eventually, after a long and traumatic overland journey through the mountains with his brother and a cousin, they achieved their freedom. The other two acted as his escorts and most likely were quite prepared to give up their own lives for their superior-minded relation; all brave people. They must have had good contacts helping them to cross from Iran into Turkey. Once there, they wouldn't have had too much trouble at the subsequent borders. They came via Istanbul, into Bulgaria and from there to Zagreb and on to Milan. The Italians tipped the wink to the Swiss when they realized that the travellers were 'unusual'. At the Italian-Swiss border, when the Iranians were no longer in fear of being arrested or refused entry, the defectors declared their wishes. The Swiss Embassy in Bern was informed, as was *Fedpol* – The Federal Office Police headquarters. Fedpol is responsible for coordinating Swiss and foreign police forces and controls the internal Intelligence agency. As you can imagine it's a very tricky and sensitive situation, both politically and from the humanitarian aspect." Guy cleared his throat before continuing.

"On arrival in Switzerland, with little luggage, not much money and unsuitable clothes for this climate, the three travel-weary men bought inexpensive, warm coats." Oliver started to speak, but Guy held up a hand to stop him.

"Yes, you have it in one. The garments they bought were three similar thick grey duffle coats. Actually dressing identically probably saved this person's life. They had in fact been tailed. The local 'Cantonal' police were instructed to take the men on to Montreux. At the police station there, by the lake, an immediate plan of action was coordinated from the control base in Bern. The cousin, the least educated and the most nervous of the group, was put on a bus travelling up into the mountains, where he was to be met and then brought here to join his relations in this safe refuge. The brother remained temporarily in Montreux. He has been extensively interviewed and is due to arrive here late this evening.

"Meanwhile our more sophisticated scientist friend went straight on to Bern, where he was taken to the Federal Office Police head-quarters. After the essential formalities had been completed, Fedpol alerted the special Enzian task force. They were ordered to discreetly escort him back to Montreux, by car, for further questioning. He was then brought on here by train. The final journey up into the mountains, on the Panoramic Express, by coincidence turned out to be the same as you had taken. The task force spirited the scientist away when, as planned, the mountain train stopped in a tunnel. He was transported by car, then snowmobile, up to this safe house. All very hush hush and extremely efficient. For obvious reasons, it was considered too risky to disembark at the station in the valley. If there had been any attempt on the man's life civilians might have become involved; including you as it happened. They might also have been spotted setting off up the mountain. In actual fact the killers, at that time, were busy with the unfortunate cousin."

Oliver, although stunned by the clandestine story, was delighted to have been proven right about the disappearing, duffle-coated man on the train. Again he looked across the room to the courageous Persian national. How could he appear so calm given the situation, uprooted and in fear for his life? Guy took a gulp of his coffee and went on.

"Zak at first was told to expect three guests; the Iranians had unwisely been staying in touch with their families as they travelled, by way of their mobiles. This, of course, made it easier for their pursuers to keep tabs on their defecting countrymen's movements. Consequently, sadly, the cousin never turned up. We think that Fedpol organized for him to go on ahead on the bus, as a red herring 'look alike', in order to protect the all-important scientist. I'm afraid that, in the higher echelons of the secret world, the cousin would have been thought expendable and of little consequence compared to our friend here."

Oliver couldn't help feeling even more sorry for the relation without the brains and wondered whether the poor scientist knew about his cousin's probable untimely end. Hopefully he wouldn't be shown the bloodied coat. That would be truly horrible. Guy went on:

"It's most likely that the relation was seen boarding the bus and was then taken at some stop on the journey. The Cantonal police are investigating and we are awaiting that info. So far, all that has been found of him is the coat that caused Rose's fall, which still has to be tested, although it's likely to be his. Also, there's the matter of the blood in the snow that you told us about, which we need to look into further."

"It's gone," said Oliver, "or been covered over; at least removed from sight. I don't think you'll find the blood, if that's what it was in the first place. Rose does have a vivid imagination."

"We'll find it if it's there to be found, don't you worry. But we'll need to be extremely discreet with these hired hatchet men around, at least until we evaluate their capabilities. Their task is to find the defecting scientist before he can divulge his knowledge or any other information that the Iranians would prefer to keep under wraps, particularly at present, with us and the whole unsettled world watching. They also know that the scientist won't immediately give away his crucial information; he's an intelligent man who will have thought long and hard about all this. He'll hold it as bargaining power to get his family out, for which you can't blame him. So the hit men think they have time enough to find the key man, probably also the other surviving family member who, although relatively unimportant, would be considered an added bonus. The fact that all three defectors bought the same coats was pure chance, but it must have thrown their pursuers into certain disarray. They couldn't be certain which of the three duffle-coated men they were pursuing was the all important scientist. Remember, they all bear the same name, have similar initials and carry very little else to distinguish them from one another. Whether or not this was intentional, it was in fact a clever move. So far..." Guy surreptitiously indicated their guest sitting quietly by the fire, "to our certain knowledge only one of this man's relations is missing."

"What about the ugly looking, duffle-coated foreigner I saw in the hotel?" asked Oliver.

"Well, yes, he could well have been one of the gang, watching for arrivals at your station. Although, if he'd been watching the trains I'd expect him to use the café nearby, not the hotel. He'd stick out like a sore thumb amongst the residents." Guy was thoughtful for a moment. "And again he probably bought the jacket when first they arrived, either in the market or at a station; these particular garments are easy to come by. Iranian people are used to the cold in winter, but they needed to blend in as much as possible with the locals."

"The man I saw certainly appeared suspicious; he was alone, out of place as you say and was definitely nervous," Olly replied, with some satisfaction. "Good Lord! I thought he gave me an odd look, but maybe he was actually watching Rose?"

"Perhaps he was," continued Guy. "Anyway, because of all this we now have another problem on our hands. The girls: they are vulnerable, especially Rose. If it was evidence of the crime that she found, she might well have been seen rummaging around. What exactly was your grey man up to in the hotel? It's important now that our other halves bow out, stay in a group, don't start publically asking questions or in any way attract attention to themselves." Oliver sat up, alarmed.

"Don't fuss!" Guy continued unfazed, "Alicia has already sent me a text, so I know roughly where they are. I have told them to return to the hotel immediately." Even so, in spite of this reassurance, Oliver could see that Guy was anxious.

"The trouble is, it's only a matter of time before these geeks realize that their quarry has disappeared. They'll wonder if the Swiss have him and at that point the girls could hold a certain bargaining power. The men will be held responsible back in their own country and could become even more desperate. So," finished Guy glancing up at Julian, "I am afraid that this particular situation could curb everybody's holiday. I'll also have to post somebody 'incognito' in the hotel. But understandably that won't go down too well with Anton and Hélène."

"I shouldn't think it will," muttered Julian. "And I don't blame them, not one bit."

"Good grief!" was all Oliver could manage, as he digested all this unwelcome information.

❄

The girls had no intention of returning to the hotel; they were thoroughly enjoying themselves, putting any problems behind them in the cool, reassuring light of day whilst they concentrated on their skiing. It was a Monday, the sun was shining for the moment and there weren't many people out, so they had the slopes almost to themselves.

Guy's rather curt text wasn't happily received, but they had stopped to read it. Then Alicia turned the mobile off. The battery was low: she'd forgotten to charge it.

"Why should we go back to the hotel? They're not even there themselves. What a cheek! I'll try to send a reply when we stop next and ask them to let us know when they arrive back at base. Then we'll consider coming down."

Adriana laughed, "Heavens, they are beginning to rather depend on us, aren't they? Just like a couple of old women. What's more, unlike you, I'm not even married yet."

"I know," Alicia answered, "but I reckon Julian is warming up to it. What do you think Rose?"

"I think that if I were Adriana I'd give him a shove."

"What do you mean? How exactly?" Adriana was bewildered.

73

"Make him jealous: with the doctor," replied Rose shortly.

"Marc...? No, I couldn't possibly. Anyway, he adores Emma and I really like her too. I like them both actually, very much."

"Well," said Rose, "she's not going to know and if she did she wouldn't be seriously bothered surely? He thinks you're sexy; that's quite obvious. It would only be a means to an end and you don't have to exactly go the whole hog. It just might work."

"Goodness what manipulation... but I think it's quite a good idea actually," agreed Alicia, giggling. "I think Emma would forgive us; it's time we had another wedding. Anyway, I'm getting cold, so how about one more run? Then let's go to the hut for something hot on the way back."

Off they went again, gliding expertly down the mountain, one after the other. None of them saw the two darkly dressed men, watching from the protecting forest as they sped by.

Half an hour later they reached the hut. It was a welcome respite. There was nobody else there and so they sat beside the fire, drinking hot glühwein and discussing Adriana's tactics to entice Julian into finally popping the question. Both Rose and Alicia readily agreed to help.

"I can't believe we are planning to be so devious, but it could be a lot of fun," said Alicia, pleased for her friend that, at last, they might manage to move Julian along in the right direction. After all it had been considered a done deal for ages. He just needed to get on with it and do the deed.

"I vote that we get them to take us dancing one night, down in the town; that would be a good opportunity to get things going, wouldn't it?" suggested Rose.

"Yes, and Adriana dances better than anybody I know," replied Alicia, smiling across at her.

"Okay, but we mustn't take it too far otherwise I shall feel really disloyal to Emma." Adriana wasn't too sure about the plan.

"Don't fret," said Rose "I honestly don't think that Julian needs too big a shove; just a gentle nudge perhaps."

The three friends had spent a really fun afternoon. It had been easy to put aside their earlier misgivings and the morning's events as they concentrated on a plan to persuade Julian into proposing marriage.

Outside, the sun was dropping fast, leaving behind a glowing, pink sky promising a clear day to follow. The eagles called to each other as they glided in the thermals high above the hut, turning and basking in the late, warm rays of the sun. The mountain was settling for night. Alicia, with a puzzled frown, was busy looking at her mobile.

"Two missed calls and my battery really is very low: it's Guy; why on earth do they want us back in such a hurry? Perhaps they have some interesting news. I suppose we'd better think about it though, as it's getting late now and, as we well know, that path does get icy." Rose wasn't listening. She was thinking about something else altogether.

"We mustn't forget to pick up the blood-stained coat on the way past."

"Oh my God! Yes, I nearly forgot," Alicia agreed. "It will save time and if Marc has got the pathology results, they'll need it to see if the DNA matches."

"Up here on this beautiful mountain, away from it all, it's really hard to believe that there could be anything nasty going on," said Rose in a quiet voice. "I have had such a great time with you two; thanks for including me."

"Not at all, Rose," answered Adriana, "we loved having you with us, didn't we Ally?" Alicia nodded enthusiastically. It had been a great afternoon's skiing as the three of them were equally skilled.

The girls left the welcome warmth of the little hut and set off once more, in line, down the tricky, narrow track through the forest. Rose was ahead as she knew where to find the coat. The others followed a little way behind, mindful of the black, icy patches. Suddenly, in front, Rose stopped abruptly and shot sideways off the path. As the others approached she was gesticulating wildly for them to be quiet and to move out of sight.

"What is it?" whispered Alicia drawing up beside her.

"There are two people in the wood, rummaging around in the undergrowth. Look!" They all peered from behind a tree. Sure enough there were two figures in the distance amongst the trees, searching for something.

"That's just where the coat is hidden: they're looking for it, I'm certain of it," breathed Rose in a shocked undertone.

"You're right, they're really busy, bashing around with their sticks. Luckily they haven't seen us, but what do we do now? This is the only way down from here," Adriana murmured.

"I vote we wait awhile and watch," Alicia suggested. "This is turning into one interesting situation. Whoever are these people?"

"I don't know, but I think it's probably best they don't see us. What do you think?"

Rose was shivering.

"They could be here for ages though and I don't know about you, but I'm getting cold." Rose wished she'd put on another layer of clothing.

"Well, we could take off our skis and try to find another way home, in which case we might well get lost, or we can wait a bit longer and hope that they give up and go. The light is fading fast and we're a bit stuck without a torch," Alicia added a little nervously.

"They will go," replied Rose, more positively. "As soon as they find the coat they are bound to leave and… they're in exactly the right place."

"I hope you're right," breathed Adriana almost to herself, feeling the cold beginning to find its way in and creep down the back of her neck.

* * *

CHAPTER 8

"WHERE the bloody hell are they?" Guy was unusually rattled, as it was unlike Alicia not to answer his messages. He wished now that, before he'd left his wife earlier, he'd given her a little more information regarding the situation. The three men had returned to the hotel and were sitting once again in the room off the reception area.

"The damn phone's run down and the other two have left their mobiles behind as well, that's what's happened. They're all together; they'll be fine," Julian answered, sounding more confident than he actually felt. He just hoped that the girls were already down safely having a drink in a bar, somewhere in the village.

"I'll ring Otto," said Guy, "and see if they're in the hut on the black cut." He took out his phone and punched in the numbers. He could hear it ringing eerily in the obviously empty hut: and he experienced an apprehension that in the past had seldom let him down.

Hélène came across to ask them if they wanted anything to drink. Should she call the waiter?

"Ah Hélène, *grüezi*, hello, no, I think that we are fine thanks: we're actually just waiting for our women and they're late back. I suppose you wouldn't have any idea what their plans were today?" Julian could tell that Guy's air of nonchalance contained an undertone of extreme alarm.

"Well," said Hélène, "as a matter of fact we had rather an odd morning here in the hotel. Another of our guests arrived who, funnily enough, Alicia and Adriana had met before; a young doctor, who I think also knows you and Julian. Unfortunately, on his journey here the poor man had the unpleasant task of dealing with a suicide on the railway line, just the other side of the village. Such a thing in this part of the world is unheard of." Hélène was obviously still very much affected by this shocking event happening so near her idyllic hotel. The three men were silenced, looking from one to the other, their minds working overtime. Guy recovered himself first.

"God! What an awful thing to happen. Who was the man and who is the doctor?"

"The man was a foreigner, probably Middle Eastern, they said; that's all we could find out, for the moment. I suppose that they would have to identify the man and inform his family before they can give out any more information to the rest of us. The doctor is called Marc Neilson."

"A Middle Easterner, was it?" Guy glanced fleetingly at Julian and raised an eyebrow. "How curious…" then he quickly changed the subject, "but how brilliant, what an extraordinary thing, Marc Neilson being here: yes, they are a great couple. We all met the year before last in Greece and then went back for their wonderful and very 'Greek' wedding in the autumn. Is Emma with him now?"

"No," replied Hélène, her cheeks warm. She had to think quickly and she wasn't too good at telling fibs. "She'll be here in a few days. Someone was ill and she couldn't find another person to take over the office in England."

"Well, well, well. What a coincidence," said Julian, genuinely pleased to have two more friends joining them. Hélène went on to tell them all that she knew of the girls' movements for the day. She remembered that they went for a walk with Marc after breakfast, because she'd seen them all go out together. He had to go to the police station to make a statement in the afternoon and, as far as she knew, the girls had gone off skiing. Why, was there a problem?

"No, no not at all. It's just that we'd go and join them if we knew where they were. Alicia's phone has run down and the other two, I expect, have left them behind in their rooms."

Hélène moved off to greet some newly-arrived guests and the men sat silently, considering this latest piece of news, until she was out of earshot. They certainly weren't about to unsettle their hostess with further speculation. Oliver spoke first. He'd gone quite pink in the face, after an exhilarating day in the cold air, followed now by the warmth inside.

"It's Rose you're concerned about, isn't it?" he asked, wishing for the umpteenth time that he had insisted that she keep her mobile with her this morning. The trouble was that she had been half asleep when he left, but he should have left a note to remind her to take it with her.

"No, it's actually Alicia who fusses me more. She and Adriana have had adventures before." Guy glanced across at Julian, who was sitting frowning in the chair opposite. "Those two are quite capable of doing their own little bit of investigating given the chance. With this latest development, if Rose has told them about the blood in the snow and about finding the coat when she fell on the track, then they might well have started sniffing around, drawing unwanted attention..."

Julian interrupted. "That's it, that's where they are! I'll bet they have gone to look for the blood-stained coat."

"You're right. They might have gone there; but something else must have happened for them to have stayed out so late," answered Guy getting up and taking out his mobile again. "I'll just check that the snowmobiles are still where we left them; then let's go and find them!"

They set off up the road, as they had earlier at dawn, to the place where they'd left the machines. It was almost dark now. All the skiers were in, but the piste bashers hadn't yet started their evening's work, preparing the slopes for the next day. An owl, it's huge, round eyes glowing against the darkening sky, flew out above their heads, making Oliver jump. It was bitterly cold and although the sky still held the faint, coloured aftermath of another spectacular sunset, the light was fading fast. Oliver sensed a heightening of tension. The other two men weren't going to let on, but he knew that they too were worried.

❋

"They aren't going to give up easily, are they? I wonder who on earth these people are," puzzled Alicia.

"Look, look! They're getting torches out," exclaimed Rose beginning to shiver.

"I vote we leave our skis hidden and head on back up to the hut before we freeze to death." Adriana muttered. "If we're lucky, there might still be someone there clearing up. We'll never find another way out now that it's dark and we can't exactly ski nonchalantly past these creeps as, whoever they are, they're not up to any good. I can't believe that Rose and I forgot our bloody mobiles and that yours has run down Ally; have another go and see if it will at least send a message."

The mobile just blinked unhelpfully, so the three friends hid their skis from sight in the undergrowth, then in the gathering gloom began to pick their way slowly back up the way they had come. The track was hazardous, becoming very slippery and their ski boots were difficult to walk in.

They didn't speak again until the torches were mere pin pricks behind them in an otherwise black forest. The moon, appearing through the trees, was a relief. It lit their way, casting eerie shadows across the path as they trudged on.

"At least I'm warm again now," whispered Rose. Alicia had stopped and was peering ahead straining her eyes into the distance.

"Yes, so am I," agreed Adriana.

"It's alright, we don't have to whisper any more," said Alicia, "but I'm afraid we do have a problem; there's no light ahead. Otto must have gone home by now and the hut will be all locked up."

"Well then, we'll just have to break in," answered the ever practical Adriana.

"And there's bound to be a telephone we can use too," added Rose for good measure. They tramped on, thankful when the welcoming little hut finally came into full view, silhouetted against the opalescent moon. Alicia tried the door. As expected it was solid and firmly shut. They moved round to the window.

"It's going to be easier said than done to break in: the windows are all double glazed. Let's go around the back see if we can unearth a brick or something," suggested Adriana.

"Wait, wait! I just heard something. There's someone in there. Listen…" whispered Rose, her eyes large and shining in the moonlight. Sure enough they could hear somebody moving around inside. Adriana was sniffing the air.

"Hang on, there's a smell here that I recognize: it's cow. Listen again!" They all listened and, sure enough, they could then hear the cow bells ringing as the animals moved around inside. Alicia giggled.

"Well at least it will be warm in there. Even if we do have to pal up with the cattle for the night, we'll survive. Thank goodness it's spring… let's look for a way in."

"I've never been too keen on cows," Rose piped up in a small voice. "Not since one chased me up a tree, when I was little. I was stuck there for three hours while it ate all the apples on the ground underneath."

"You mustn't be nervous," answered Adriana, "Swiss cows are different. They're used to living closely with humans and are very people-friendly." With the others following, she went around the back to find the entrance.

"I shouldn't think this door will be locked."

It wasn't. The half door was merely secured by a latch and the top by a piece of wood through a ring. Alicia attempted to send one last message to both Marc and Guy but she couldn't tell whether or not it was successful. Then they went in to join the astonished cows.

*

Marc soon discovered that not only were the girls still out, but so also were Julian and Guy. They must all be together he decided, looking at his watch. It was late. Most likely they were all in a bar somewhere: the girls would be filling their men in with the day's events. What a relief. He would have been seriously concerned to think of them out alone, considering the outcome of the afternoon's revelations.

He was looking forward to seeing Julian and Guy again. He'd liked them both and they'd all had a great time at his and Emma's wedding. What a pity she couldn't have got away from work earlier; he was already really missing her. They'd hardly ever been apart since their marriage. Well, he'd go up and have a bath then give her a ring.

❋

Guy was concentrating on the path. Although it was reasonably well lit by the moon, it wasn't easy negotiating the narrow, bumpy track without the beam of headlights. Oliver was first to see the torches ahead. He dug Guy sharply in the ribs, pointing. Guy looked up and braked immediately. Julian, close behind, nearly collided with them.

"What the fuck...?" Guy's hand went up signalling from the front. They could all see the torches moving around, obviously searching for something, in the dark forest before them. Luckily their progress was muffled by the noise of the piste bashers which had begun their work, somewhere up on their right. The little entourage would have neither been seen nor heard.

"I reckon they are looking for the bloody coat: just a minute, there's a message come in, the mobile's vibrating; now let's just hope it's the girls..."

Guy took out his mobile, holding it discreetly; it was flashing. The other two were silent, the tension palpable while they waited.

"It's Alicia alright, but not much has come through, the signal's bad, no juice. It's hard to make sense… hang on, there's a bit more coming… 'caution, torches… in h…' That's all. They must be in the hut. They must have also seen the torches and gone back up. OK we'll have to turn around and go up the ski slope, under cover of the piste bashers, then in from the top."

✻

At almost the same time Marc, up in his room, saw his mobile flash a message. It was Alicia. He read the text and understood immediately what had happened.

There was no sign of the other two men in the hotel. It was dark, but the girls were up there alone. Perhaps he should return to the police station… no, by the time he'd tried to explain the situation it would take too long. Somehow, he must get up the mountain himself, to the middle station and then on to the hut. Luckily, after a previous visit, he should remember how to get there. The way across was treacherous to say the least. He just hoped that, at this time of the day, his unreliable expertise on the slopes was up to it.

✻ ✻ ✻

CHAPTER 9

THE girls had been talking softly together and had almost become resigned to the reality that they would have to manage a night with the cows. Rose had even chipped in, saying that she actually didn't think the cows would really mind if she went to the loo either, whereupon they had all dissolved into peels of giggles. It was quite warm and the animals, after the girls' initial intrusion, didn't seem at all bothered by their presence. They were very docile. Alicia was the first to hear the noise outside.

"Quiet, there's someone coming." Instinctively they all crouched down together against some bales of straw.

"They won't see us here if they look in. We're too far from the door."

They huddled together, trying to control their breathing, their hearts hammering and their hearing keenly tuned, as they listened to the approaching footsteps.

"It might be Guy and Julian," whispered Rose.

"No, it's only one person and I think he's on skis," answered Alicia.

"It might be the cow man," offered Rose hopefully.

"No, it's too late in the day and anyway they come on snowmobiles at this time of year."

"Well I'm scared then."

"Shh, they're nearly here."

Someone was trying the door of the hut at the main entrance.

"He's going to see our footsteps and follow them round here, so there's actually no point in trying to hide," announced Adriana practically and almost forgetting to whisper.

"Oh heavens!"

The footsteps came shuffling around the side of the building and they heard a stumbling noise followed by a very English obscenity. Adriana recognised the voice first.

"Oh my God! It's Marc! Thank goodness! Marc! Marc! We're here, in here."

They all leapt up, which threw the cows into total confusion and, not caring where they stepped and skirting around the edge, made towards the door. Marc's grinning face appeared out of the gloom.

"Hello you lot… Christ it stinks in here!"

Marc had a torch and flashed it on each of the three girls in turn. They all looked dishevelled and grubby and Rose had, unknowingly, very thoroughly coated both ski boots with cow muck. The curious animals studied the newcomer then, deciding he was no threat either, continued their chewing.

"Well!" said Marc, opening the door and squeezing inside "and I thought that you lot were supposed to be on a romantic holiday." In spite of the alarming situation, he just couldn't keep the amused grin off his face.

"Alright, you can stop making fun of us now," said Rose crossly, brushing the straw from her clothes, in a rather pathetic attempt in view of her unsavoury feet, to make herself presentable. "What I want to know is the results of the pathology test." She snatched the torch from Marc and shone it on his face.

"Tell us then. I can see by your expression that you know the answer and you wouldn't have come all the way up here if it's not what I think it is either!" Marc immediately became serious, grabbed the torch back and shone it on Rose's pink, shining features.

"Yes, you were right: it was human blood and matched that of the so-called suicide case." They were all silent as they took in the information. Marc continued, "I was really worried. I should never have let you go out skiing on your own. What happened exactly? Why are you in here? I only got fragments of a message on my mobile."

Alicia recounted the afternoon's happenings since leaving the hotel, finishing with their becoming trapped on the icy path in the forest, while two strangers appeared to be searching for the blood-stained duffle coat, which they'd been on their way to collect.

"Well, I suppose I'd better ring for assistance to get us all out of... wait, listen! I think I can hear an engine and it's heading in this direction." They all stopped speaking, straining their ears to hear.

"It's coming from above us. Oh Lord! Here we go again." Alicia grabbed Rose protectively by the arm and Marc squeezed Adriana's shoulder for reassurance.

"It's two machines," he whispered, "How many men were in the wood?"

"Two," squeaked Rose in a tight voice.

"What's Guy or Julian's mobile numbers? Can you remember?" Alicia seized Marc's mobile, punched in the numbers, then held it to her ear.

"It's ringing... no answer. Come on... Where are they? I'll try Julian's then the hotel." But there wasn't time. The fast-moving snowmobiles had almost arrived.

The cows backed away and let their unexpected visitors pass as they retreated to the furthest corner of the barn. Rose was now shivering with fright and also trying hard to hide the fact that her teeth were chattering. Alicia picked up a brick from under the window ledge and Adriana a weighty piece of wood. Rose, feeling inadequate, secured a piece of chain wedged in a manger. Marc, thinking 'how the hell am I going to deal with this particular emergency', quickly indicated for the girls to hide behind the bales of straw and to keep quiet. Then, settling the torch on the highest straw bale, quickly looked around for a weapon himself: there was a pitchfork hanging between two hooks on a piece of wood by the door. He manoeuvred around the milling animals, grabbed the fork and began piling the straw up against the girls' hiding place.

The engines outside were cut and there was a sudden silence, broken only by a low murmuring of voices and the occasional deep resounding clonk of a bell, as a cow moved its head to feed. The smell of the dung hung heavy in the air. Rose vowed that she'd never be mean about cows again. They offered a certain comfort in worrisome circumstances.

The new arrivals were also listening. Then Marc knew that whoever they were had noticed the footsteps outside and were following the tracks around the hut. He could hear the scrunch of their feet in the snow. In a very short time now he would be discovered: keep cool, at all costs; keep cool, he thought as he started whistling and continued to move the straw around, shaking it expertly. The top of the stable door opened and another powerful torch beam flooded the barn.

"Jesus! What on earth are you doing in there?" enquired an astonished Guy.

*

The problem was that they couldn't all get on the two snowmobiles. Two people had to stay behind. Marc offered to stay, as did Adriana who managed a surreptitious wink in the direction of Alicia before the first party left to make their way downhill. Alicia would have caught her meaning and would have played on the current situation to the full. It had been quite apparent that Julian hadn't exactly been comfortable with the idea of Adriana being left alone in the dark with Marc. The weather had worsened and it was starting to snow again. It would be a good forty minutes before their expected return.

"Well," said Marc, as he and Adriana settled themselves close together on a straw bale. "So far it's certainly been a most interesting day, hasn't it?"

"Yes, and some of it we could happily have done without, I can tell you," she answered. "Especially walking in ski boots all the way up here: which reminds me, I hope they remember to pick up our skis." Adriana looked around at the cows, staring as they munched. "I must say, although we could certainly do with a spray bottle of fresh air, our hosts here have really made us very welcome, considering our rather rude intrusion!"

Marc laughed. He had a very infectious laugh and Adriana remembered that it was his sense of fun which had drawn her to him when they had first met in Greece two summers before. It really wasn't going to be at all difficult to make Julian just a little jealous and she was sure that Emma, had she known, wouldn't have minded, once she knew the reason. She just wouldn't let it go too far.

They sat in the dark talking quietly together. Marc recounted his experience that afternoon at the police station. Then he told Adriana how he had managed to get a lift up the mountain to the middle station, in a cable car taking supplies on up to the restaurant at the top. Adriana was just about to launch forth on her theory regarding their present situation when she stopped abruptly, listening acutely again.

"It's them already returning, can you hear…?"

"Yes, but it's too quick and it's a single machine," answered Marc. "Our friends can't possibly have gone all the way down to the bottom and back in, what is it…" he shone the torch quickly on his watch face "only thirty minutes? I'm afraid it's more likely to be those people you saw in the wood. They would have seen the lights on in the hut and then heard Otto leave for the night. They might even have seen you making your way up here and followed. Let's just hope they're lost or at least harmless. But we need a plan of action fast, to both stall for time and to throw them off balance… OK take your jacket off and undo your ski pants! Quick."

"For God's sake… is this really necessary? Guy might just have forgotten something," giggled Adriana understanding Marc's intention and even amused, in spite of their vulnerability. She knew there was mutual attraction between them and if by some miracle it was the others returning, this would definitely give Julian something to think about!

"Yes, sorry but can't think of anything else. Come on hurry up, try and look a bit more déshabillé too."

The snowmobile was arriving from a different direction, from through the forest below. They could hear it floundering through the deep snow, the engine stuttering a little, as if in need of maintenance. It was definitely a different machine.

"Right it could be the cow man, but in case it's not, imagine the scent of your favourite flowers and let's make it look good. I just hope the others will soon be on their way back."

"Oh, they will be, don't you worry." Adriana said with feeling as she remembered the look on Julian's face when he'd had to leave her here.

Marc pulled Adriana to him, removed her jacket, roughed up her hair and, finding her mouth, began to kiss her with abandon. 'If these people really are up to no good, this could just possibly defuse the situation or, if they turn out to be no threat,' Adriana was thinking, 'I shall just have one extremely jealous boyfriend on my hands.' Either way it was the best option, so she opened her mouth and entered into her role enthusiastically. She'd often wondered what it would be like to be kissed by this man.

The visitors arrived at the hut and once more, starting at the front of the building, began their inspection. It certainly was not their friends or the cow man. The kiss went on, deepening as the adrenalin pumping around their bodies aroused heightened signals of physical need. Marc's hands began to wander naturally, finding their way underneath Adriana's jersey to her soft bare skin. As he touched her breast she instantly responded, feeling the sensual rush within her begin to rise, wanting more.

The men were coming closer around the side of the building. They were speaking some unknown dialect. It sounded like a rough form of Arabic. This was extremely unnerving and not a good omen. 'Unless I play my cards right now we could be in a lot of trouble.' Marc surmised. He had to keep his head, cool it and delay things to give the others time to return.

In spite of their strange and disturbing situation, Marc was struggling to keep this planned diversionary ruse with Adriana in control. He'd always been attracted to her. His own desire for her was escalating, heightened probably by genuine fear. Marc was unused to unprovoked violence and wasn't at all sure how to prepare himself for this possibility, but he was determined to protect this brave girl whatever the cost. These people might already be responsible for a murder, in which case they weren't going to harm Adriana, not if he had anything to do with it.

The newcomers were right outside now. The cows moved over towards the door, hoping perhaps that more fodder was about to appear and shielding the two in hiding. Adriana, lying back across the bales, her clothes loosened, was almost beyond thought. Perhaps the people would just go away when they realized there were animals in here. She no longer felt frightened and more than anything now she wanted this man to make love to her, even if it wasn't in the most romantic setting. Marc's free hand found its way lower, the other supporting her head as the kissing continued. She mustn't make a noise as, one way or another, their future was about to be determined. If only they'd just go. There was silence except for the cows. Then they heard low voices. Adriana suddenly remembered that their ski sticks were propped outside. Oh God! a dead giveaway. Then for the third time the top door was flung open. As the cows scattered, the dark shed was thrown into light once more from a powerful beam, revealing their two writhing bodies in the corner. Two dark heads peered in cautiously, conferred a moment, then yanked open the bottom half of the door and came in slamming it shut behind them.

"Let me do the talking. Don't do anything!" whispered Marc authoritively, sitting up and feigning surprise. One hand was reaching for the brick that he had placed in readiness beside him, the other held protectively around Adriana who was trying to reassemble both her thoughts and her clothes.

The torch shone directly down on the two of them, making it hard to see the strangers behind the light. But as the two intruders advanced across the space between them it was clear that they were hostile as both held guns. One weapon covered Marc and the other Adriana. The torch came to a halt resting on her disordered appearance. The older man, who seemed in charge, stared in amazed silence, his eyes darting from one part of Adriana's anatomy to another. Marc thought it was time to interrupt the man's obvious train of thought. Here his training as a doctor helped him to keep outwardly calm, but he found himself feeling angry. No way was this man going to touch Adriana in the way that was intended.

"Hello, who are you? Are you lost?" he asked politely, straightening up, then feigning surprise and attempting to sound forceful. "Would you mind putting those guns away? My girlfriend and I are unarmed. We have no need for fire-arms in these mountains."

"*Saket sho!*" The distracted man spat, swiping his hand across in front of him, "No speak, *vaystah.*"

He barked some orders at his partner, indicating he should cover Marc then slid his eyes back to Adriana. He licked his lips, snorted in delight and moved closer, indicating that she raise her jersey further to reveal her breasts. The younger individual coughed, unsure of his direction. Marc sat down again and tightly gripped the brick close at his side. Adriana, also angry in shock, shook her head in defiance.

"No way, you ugly piece of shit," she muttered. The man snarled in annoyance. 'Shit' was a word he understood in any language. He conferred again with his companion whose eyes darted anxiously from one prisoner to the other. Then to Marc's horror the older man made his intentions quite clear as he started to unbuckle his belt.

"Slow it down," he whispered, as the foreigners spoke together, "The others will be here soon... I hope," he finished under his breath.

The younger man raised his gun, pointing it at Marc's head as he had obviously been told, gesticulating for him to move away from Adriana. The other was now undoing his trousers and whistling between his teeth as with glinting, lust filled eyes he studied his quarry. Adriana had hold of the piece of wood behind her back. These people were the remnants of God's earth and she'd fight to the death before she'd let this disgusting old man touch her. She sat watching his lecherous face and then became aware that they also had an audience, as the cows had now turned and, making a semi-circle around them, were all watching with curious, kind eyes. This suddenly struck her as absurd. She felt her mouth begin to quiver and a weak giggle escaped her lips followed by a burst of nervous laughter. The senior man, baffled, hesitated and stopped his planned assault.

"What on earth do you find funny about our present situation?" Marc shot at her, suppressing a grin himself, realizing that the frenzied foreign men were looking from one to the other, waving their guns around, bewildered by Adriana's behaviour.

"I was just thinking that these poor cows have never had such an interesting time and that now, on top of everything else, they are about to witness my rape."

Adriana then dissolved into helpless, hysterical laughter and Marc, seeing the reaction this was causing, joined her. The men, unnerved by this unexpected turn of events, became even more annoyed. The cows, sensing such unrest, were now moving and shoving, one against the other. The younger man looked behind him, knocked into the rump of a shifting cow and the gun went off. There was a sharp crack as the bullet split the wood somewhere above their heads. He dropped the weapon, and had his hand trodden on trying to retrieve it from the dirty straw. The yelp of pain only provoked more confusion. The other brute, now in charge of the torch, was shouting and cursing, avoiding the milling animals as best he could. When a cow filled the space between themselves and their assailants, Marc seized his moment: he grabbed Adriana's arm and crouching low they managed to cross to the other corner of the barn where they remained still and hidden, protected by the manger above them. Their bells now clonking and clanging, the agitated herd lurched around the two frightened, shouting men.

"I think that with any luck they're trying to get out, before they're trampled on," Marc whispered in her ear, from their place flat against the wall.

Sure enough, one of the foreigners eventually managed to make it as far as the entrance, followed by the second man, now screaming in panic. The door opened then shut and they could hear their two adversaries slump against it in relief. It was then that Adriana heard the distant sound of engines. Julian and Guy were well on their way and approaching fast.

"Well," said Marc as he heard the two foreigners hurriedly leave, "who would ever have thought that a bunch of cows would save our lives... and you were brilliant?" He turned towards Adriana.

"So were you. Thank you." She answered without hesitation.

The release of tension was palpable. Her face was close and she was smiling. He couldn't resist that smile and she, abandoning all thoughts of self control, entered wholeheartedly into the enjoyment of one last kiss. After all, they had just managed to extract themselves safely from one potentially horrendous ordeal, the outcome of which might have left them both either damaged or dead.

* * *

CHAPTER 10

"WHAT exactly did happen up there in the hut?" asked Alicia of her friend later that evening. The men and Rose had gone ahead to the bar.

"What on earth do you mean, Ally? We told you what happened." Adriana answered perhaps a little truculently, averting her face and waving goodnight to the staff in the dining room; to divert attention away from herself perhaps, thought Alicia.

"You know perfectly well what I mean: with Marc of course, it's quite obvious that something else happened between you two." Alicia took hold of her friend's arm to stop her walking on. Adriana stopped, turned and, sighing deeply, looked Alicia straight in the face.

"Oh Ally, it's hard to explain really, it's just that... well we were only putting on a show and, in the heat of the moment, it just sort of turned into 'for real', but only for a minute. That's all. The ambiance wasn't exactly conducive to an act of mad passion now was it? Anyway, don't worry about it. It's not going any further. Emma is due out soon, she's my friend too and I wouldn't dream of upsetting things. It really was just one of those unexpected happenings which, given the circumstances, got a bit out of hand, that's all... honestly." Adriana smiled weakly adding. "But I shall never again mind the smell of cows, I can tell you!"

Alicia grinned back somewhat knowingly and walked on, saying over her shoulder, "OK... well, it certainly did the trick as far as Julian was concerned. When he saw you in that somewhat dishevelled state he was as jealous as hell. I heard him discussing the whole episode with Guy, just before dinner. Guy made a big mistake in teasing him and Julian didn't like that at all. Well done Ari, very well done indeed, on all counts. It's worked out just as we intended, but we could have done without all that frightening drama of course. I would have been terrified: I'm surprised you're not a nervous wreck."

"Nonsense!" muttered Adriana, catching up and trying to appear unfazed, "of course you wouldn't have been terrified. After the initial shock of being faced with the weaponry, I realized that they were probably just as scared as we were. I never really thought they'd use the guns and when I understood what the lecherous older man had in mind... well that actually made me furious. They were in fact a miserable pair of wimps who were shaking in their shoes and frightened of the cows. Besides which, they couldn't really have coped with another couple of bodies up there on the mountain, now could they?" Alicia stopped and turned around to look her friend in the eye.

"No, I suppose not, but don't tell me you didn't enjoy your little escapade with Marc, because I can tell by your face that you did... didn't you?"

"Yes," replied Adriana quietly, eyes twinkling. "You're right, I did very much enjoy my little dalliance with Marc in the cow shed, especially after all the scary stuff was over and," she winked, "I shan't pretend to you otherwise!"

"Hum, thought so. Well you'd better make the most of the situation with Julian then. I shall just drop a gentle hint to Guy, knowing that it will be passed on. Now that's sorted out, let's catch the others up shall we?" Alicia marched on, a smug smile on her face, with Adriana almost running to keep up.

"Now Ally, be careful, you won't overdo it will you?"

"Don't be so silly, of course not. You know me, I'll be really discreet, I promise!" As they joined the others it was quite obvious to Rose what the two girls had been talking about and she was sorry to have missed out!

Marc wondered what Adriana was thinking. She was quite flushed and sparkly eyed after their ordeal, yet she didn't seem to be in any way embarrassed, although at dinner she wouldn't quite catch his eye. He was feeling a little guilty for having enjoyed kissing her so much, especially that last embrace, when he knew they were safe. It could easily have led to much more in a different situation. Yet he thought that it was probably lucky the others had arrived back when they did.

He liked Adriana well enough yet he knew that during their ordeal it had merely been the nervous rush of adrenalin which had been responsible for their instantaneous sexual arousal. It had seemed like a good idea at the time and had definitely defused the situation as he had intended: but perhaps he should say something to her if the opportunity arose, as he didn't want any bad vibes hanging around when Emma arrived at the weekend. He just couldn't wait to have her with him again and, thank God, this should all be in the past by then.

❅

Emma was feeling extremely pleased with herself. Liz in the office had come up trumps. She had found someone brilliant to help in her travel agency while Emma was away. She could have followed Marc out almost immediately but had taken one more day, for the doctor's appointment, to leave things organized as best as possible in London and to get her hair cut. Marc was going to get the surprise of his life when she turned up in Switzerland several days before she was expected.

She sat in the airport departure lounge, wondering if she had forgotten to do anything back at home: iron off, cooker, window locks etc; at the same time gazing around at her fellow passengers. Which one would she get next to her? She hoped not the overly large Frenchman who looked as if he'd tucked into too many long, lucrative, business lunches. There wouldn't be much room for her if she was sat next to him. Several more men, with their tell-tale brief cases, either read newspapers or checked for last minute emails on their lap tops. There were the obvious more well-to-do skiers, all noisy and in holiday mode, a few children and various older people, some single, perhaps returning to their families. Emma was looking forward to a comfortable British Airways, Club Class, flight which was one of her travel agency perks that she very much appreciated.

They boarded on time and everybody settled quickly, anticipating an easy journey. Just as they were expecting to taxi out to the runway Emma, sitting at the back of the Club Class section, noticed a slight commotion up in front. The plane door reopened and the pilot announced that he was sorry for the slight delay, but they were waiting for three late passengers. A sigh went around the compartment and several of the businessmen checked their watches in mild annoyance. Emma watched with interest, as everybody else did, to see who was important enough to keep the flight waiting. In a very short time, a smart young woman appeared through the doorway, accompanied by a possible husband. He in turn was followed closely by an obvious secretary, carrying a black case. The man looked vaguely familiar. Political people, or at any rate somebody she'd seen on the television or in the newspapers, thought Emma losing interest. They soon sat down, the door was once more secured and the plane immediately taxied out to the runway. Emma returned to the crossword in her newspaper.

The time spent in the air was all too short. Emma was thoroughly enjoying sitting still for once, but they were soon descending and on final approach for Geneva. In spite of the short delay at Heathrow they were on time. Emma checked her watch. If she was lucky and her luggage arrived quickly, she would catch the next train to Montreux. Sure enough the belt was rotating as she arrived in the baggage hall with the Club Class luggage appearing first.

The fast train to Montreux via Lausanne left promptly as always. Emma had even had the time to buy some lunch in the station – a baguette sandwich and a take-away coffee. Once aboard she heaved a sigh of relief and allowed herself to relax. There was something about rushing for trains or buses that always slightly undermined her confidence. She supposed it was all about not being in control or in charge, as you are when you drive yourself: but now the main part of the journey was over. The little mountain train that climbed up the mountain from Montreux always waited, besides which the Swiss rail system was so punctual that the connection shouldn't be a problem.

In Lausanne several people got into their carriage, including two roughly attired men, shifty-looking individuals; Emma had noticed them walking up alongside the train, before boarding, as if looking for someone. They scowled at Emma as they went past, knocking into her with the small hold-all which one of them carried. She held her bag tight into her side, glancing up at her luggage, checking it remained where a fellow passenger had placed it for her. There had been various stories of people being mugged here as the train waited to commence its onward journey and Emma was not about to become one of them. The two boorish men went and sat in the row immediately in front of her. She caught a whiff of fried food and garlic clinging to their clothes. Emma considered moving further back, then came to the conclusion that it just wasn't worth the struggle as she'd have to hump her luggage with her and it wasn't too long now before they would arrive at Montreux, where she had to change train.

With typical Swiss organization, they arrived in Montreaux on time. Emma, and several of her fellow travellers, left the main-line train, crossed platforms and boarded the smaller mountain train. Now on the last leg of her journey Emma sat gazing out of the window, as ever entranced by the winter wonderland outside. It was nearly dark and as the train gained altitude it started to snow, adding yet another covering to the previous untouched blanket of pure white. Marc had told her that there had been a massive dump but she'd seldom seen as much as this on the way up to the ski valley. She looked around to see if others were appreciating the scenery outside as much as she was. There weren't many people in her compartment.

Emma stood up to retrieve her passport from her jacket pocket on the rack. As she twisted around to reach up she noticed, a few rows in front, the man who had delayed the aircraft at Heathrow. He was bent forward, talking discreetly with someone opposite. Emma leant sideways, curious to see if the other two members of the trio were travelling with him. But no; they were strangers. A rather nervous-looking Arabic man sat diagonally opposite and two men, in identical suits, occupied the other two of the four seats. They could have been police escorts, Emma thought. Perhaps the likely politician was actually a government minister of some sort: he had an air of understated importance hanging about him. I wonder where they're going, puzzled Emma. They were obviously all together. As she stood she felt other eyes watching her and, glancing round behind her, saw the same ugly duo from the last train. One of them looked up, caught her eye, smirked slightly, then slid his eyes back to his friend, who was fingering an un-smoked cigarette and coughing nervously.

Weird, thought Emma as an unwelcome cold shiver, like lingering icy fingers, slithered down her spine. She decided to put her coat back on and then ducked quickly into her seat, thankfully hidden from the uncouth couple behind. They were whispering and kept getting up and moving about, restlessly. Probably having to go out for forbidden cigarettes, thought Emma, hoping they'd get caught and determinedly trying to ignore them.

Emma sat back to concentrate instead on her immediate future. The baby, which Marc didn't even know about, was the main reason for her delay in joining him. She'd had to see the doctor, to have her pregnancy confirmed. She looked out again from the train window at the white, wintry scene. The skiing would be absolutely brilliant, although this year she'd have to take it carefully. Not that she minded, not one little bit. Emma placed her hands protectively across her stomach. She just couldn't wait to see her husband's face when she walked in and she was longing, in the privacy of their bedroom, to give him her news. He would, she knew, be thrilled at the prospect of becoming a father.

It was all arranged with Hélène, who was going to hide her somewhere in the hotel, until he had just gone in to dine with the others. Emma was so excited when

Marc had texted her to tell her they were all there. She was very much looking forward to catching up with Alicia and Adriana again and their other halves. They had all had so much fun over the period of her wedding to Marc, two years before in Greece. It was a lovely time to remember. As she began to relax once more, Emma began to feel quite sleepy, for it had been an early start when she left London that morning. Perhaps she could allow herself to doze off, just for a few minutes. The ticket inspector would awaken her should she sleep too long: they always checked carefully at each of the little stations. They seemed to remember where everybody was headed.

*

Emma awoke, with a start, as the train suddenly lurched to a stop in a tunnel. The lights inside had momentarily failed and there was an eerie silence. All she could hear was the machinery straining and clicking as if it had been brought to a halt with a huge effort. Something was wrong.

Then, all at once, pandemonium let loose: somebody shouted in English and swore, there were sounds of a struggle; a gun went off twice, followed by an ominous thud, then a door slammed. Emma immediately ducked down, aware that bodies were moving around aggressively from both behind and in front of her. The lights flickered and died again giving only a mere glimpse of chaos. Emma hadn't dared raise her head above her seat. The atmosphere was charged with terror. A woman was now crying out in alarm and she could hear people running on the gravel alongside the track. Perhaps she should try and get out but she couldn't see well enough in the dark; anyway which way should she go? Someone in there had a gun and had already fired it twice.

A harsh, guttural, foreign dialect was being spoken urgently, just beside her. She guessed it was a Middle-Eastern language and probably from the creepy couple who had been sitting behind her.

The next thing Emma knew, someone was grabbing both her arms and roughly thrusting her to her feet, while another, as he snatched her bag away, was shoving her forward. These people were robbing her. She tried to fend off her assailants and caught one in the face with her elbow, but she had not the strength to fight off two and soon found herself being propelled, reluctantly, along the passage. Why? What else did they want from her? As they neared the door Emma suddenly realized that they intended to take her outside with them.

Now, very frightened at the thought of being made to leave the train against her own free will, she tried to catch hold of the upright seats as they pushed her along, to curtail their progress. At every given opportunity she kicked at her unseen attackers as hard as she could and at least had the satisfaction of hearing a yelp or two of pain as her foot connected.

They had a torch, but it only flickered on and off at intervals and Emma was fleetingly aware of people cowering in their seats to either side. The dim emergency lights on the floor merely suggested an exit route to follow and only vaguely lit her feet. She shouted her name out loud and that she was English, hoping that someone might absorb this information and pass it on, but before she could say more she was slapped hard across the mouth by the thug in front. The blow made her head spin but at the same time she felt fury surging up through her body; these maniacs were cowards for hitting an unarmed woman.

Emma realized that she was wedged firmly between the two monsters who had been sitting behind her. Even in the partial light she knew it was them by the distinctive odour of garlic. The close proximity of their bodies gave off the stench of stale sweat. The smell of fear, she surmised, trying not to gag. She had no means of escape. Why didn't someone help her? She felt something hard and cold stuck into her back. For the moment, Emma knew that she had no choice but to comply with their demands.

✳

Back at the hotel, all was tranquil. The men had stayed late at the bar, discussing the recent events. Before they went up to bed, the girls had been given a watered-down version of the episode and been told nothing at all about what had actually taken place in the retreat at the top of the mountain. A truncated story, involving an illegal immigrant, had been concocted. Both Oliver and Marc had been sworn to secrecy as to the identity of the Iranian in the safe house and the demise of his unfortunate cousin.

Adriana and Alicia were fully aware that there was much more to the story than they had been told. With plenty of experience from past adventures they were quite content to step back and let their men take control. Guy and Julian were well qualified to do so. Hopefully now the whole matter would be taken over by the relevant authorities and they would be allowed to resume their holidays, to which they were all looking forward.

Marc had his own misgivings. Adriana and Alicia seemed happy enough now to let Julian and Guy handle things and take the lead. But he was sure that Rose remained unconvinced by the story she'd been told.

Guy also realized that Rose was going to be hard to convince, but he hoped that his wife and her friend would help convert her to their way of thinking.

Marc had been just great on all fronts and, as a doctor, he was well aware of the need for confidentiality. Oliver, on the other hand, was another matter; he knew more and had obviously entered whole-heartedly into the jaunt up the mountain. He was tough, intelligent and quite capable of working things out for himself. Oliver could prove hard to keep out of any following action, now that he had been initiated. Zak had already informed Guy that the other surviving Iranian was on his way to join his relative in the safe house up the mountain, while their future was being discussed.

Rose was decidedly unhappy. She knew perfectly well that she'd been told a cock-and-bull story and she had no intention of letting the matter drop. After all, it was she who'd found the blood in the snow in the first place. Besides which, after her adventure with the girls and Marc she was determined to get to the bottom of the whole saga. She would just have to find things out for herself.

Both Alicia and Adriana seemed content to step back now, get on with their holiday and their efforts to persuade Julian into popping the question. But Rose wasn't.

Maybe Oliver would help her; he seemed to be well into the swing of the investigation, although he hadn't been at all keen to tell her anything about their contrived day's skiing. What had they actually been up to that day? Where had they really gone? And why was even Olly unable to divulge?

She now thought that, in spite of and because of the little information she'd been fed, Julian and Guy were definitely Secret Service people, sworn to secrecy. But she needed to know for sure. She felt quite let down by Oliver for not wishing to enlighten her further. So Rose had decided to get her own back and, somewhat childishly, to reject his amorous advances when later that night they went to bed.

* * *

CHAPTER 11

EMMA, emerging from a semi-conscious state with a splitting headache, was vaguely aware that she was frightened. There was greyness all around her, discomfort and extreme cold. She didn't dare move and momentarily, while both her body and her brain recovered and adjusted to the reality of her shocking predicament, her memory failed her.

Dizziness set in and her upper stomach harboured a lurching feeling of fear and she knew not why. But she could see a patch of light somewhere high above her head. 'I am in a dark uncertain place,' thought Emma, 'but I must focus on that little chink of brightness as it signifies hope, which I know I have to hang on to. Where am I? What's happened to me?' She concentrated on that small piece of sky within her glazed line of vision; clouds were moving across, but with absolute quietness, not a breath or sigh of wind to be heard. A teasing flash of memory; the snow muffles sound, especially in the mountains. She peered upwards again. Yes, it was snowing and she could just make out the soft flakes falling. Emma loved the snow, often so silent and gentle, except when frenzied blizzards raged and winter storms enveloped the very highest peaks, growling their displeasure. Perhaps that's where she was, somewhere in the mountains, but where was Marc?

Emma tried to reorganize her thoughts, but some sixth sense and the headache made her realize she mustn't hurry them. She felt too weak to think and an unnatural sleep overcame her once more.

Emma awoke a short time later, colder than ever, but at least her headache had improved. Still she just lay resting, her eyes glued to the small, high up ever-brightening source of illumination. Her mind was muddled and dreamlike, searching for answers. Instinctively she felt her life was in the balance but the reason was frustratingly elusive. She could see and feel a certain amount, mostly pain, but she still couldn't remember. Her thoughts were out of control and tumbling around inside her sore head, making no sense of her situation.

'Whilst in this fragile trance-like state, I can only lie here and wonder at it all. Why am I here? All alone, cold... so cold, fearful and hurt? How has it all come about? If only I could remember. Perhaps now is the time to pray, if there is a God, or at least a higher power? There must be otherwise what would we all be here for? Someone surely must come to my aid. This situation is not of my making. That much I do know. But I will remember and I will live. I have to live.'

Suddenly her hands flew to her lower stomach. Teasing memory was slowly returning. The baby. She was having a baby; and then it all came back in a rush!

Below the waist, Emma didn't feel too bad, just stiff and bruised. It was her head that really hurt. She raised her shaking hand to gingerly inspect the wound. There was no blood but a huge bump where she'd been hit on the back of her skull. Her face, where she'd been slapped, was just as painful: more if anything. It stung like hell.

Deciding that neither of these two blows would actually kill her and that the baby was still on board, Emma sank back against the rough wood to take stock of her unfortunate situation. Now she began to remember all that had occurred before she had passed out. Miraculously so far, she thought that she had suffered no serious damage. How she had been brought to this place she had no idea. None too gently judging by her tender body; better not to know. Thank God she'd been unconscious while they brought her here.

Everything had happened so fast. Emma had been half carried along the dimly lit gangway of the train. Someone had been shouting desperately. Thinking back now, she thought that it might have been herself, as her throat felt strained and dry. No-one else had moved. She'd been aware of the few other passengers hiding in their seats. The two men manhandling her towards the exit were waving their guns around threateningly and there was a body on the floor. Emma had been forced to step over it. She couldn't be sure if the person was dead or not, but they hadn't moved.

In the flickering torch light she had looked around for the two heavies with their foreign charge, but they were nowhere to be seen. They had disappeared into thin air. She had thought them to be policemen; they should have helped her. It was then that she had heard doors slam somewhere outside, a car speed away and she wondered if all four had somehow managed to escape, leaving the rest of them to their fate.

The ticket inspector and the driver had appeared from the front end of the train to see what all the commotion was about and to discover who had dared to activate the emergency stop lever. They had powerful lights which, for a moment, dazzled the aggressors. The burly driver had cautiously approached. He was horrified to find his passengers in danger and, seemingly oblivious to their own vulnerability, demanded Emma's immediate release. But the gunman, still dragging her behind him, had wildly fired the weapon in the speaker's direction. Someone had screamed. Again maybe it was Emma herself. The bullet had missed its target and slammed into the infrastructure of the train. An ominous silence had followed just for a few seconds, as if everyone was holding their breath.

Then she remembered being bundled out of the train into more waiting hands, as she screamed and kicked for all she was worth. Then a dark, searing pain had engulfed her as she sank into oblivion.

Emma had only once in the past found herself to be in physical danger. On that occasion her adrenalin had been up, she'd had no time for thought before action and luckily the outcome had been successful. Today was another matter. She'd been hurt and she was cold and hungry. She was a prisoner of some person or persons unknown, but for what particular reason she had been taken she had no idea. So it was hard to decide on a plan. It was especially difficult with the added encumbrance of her unborn child to consider. The awful thing was that Marc hadn't even known that she was on her way, although Hélène would wonder where she was. She would put two and two together when word got through about the incident on the train. Surely someone would have heard her calling out her name and passed on the information to the police. If only – if only she hadn't set her heart on surprising them all. If she'd just stuck to the original schedule none of this would have happened. But no good feeling sorry for herself; she must rest and remain calm for her baby's sake, then take stock of her surroundings and assess her predicament.

Emma looked about her. She sensed it was early morning, judging by the light. She looked at her watch. It was comforting that they hadn't taken it as it was a good watch given to her by Marc soon after they'd been married. Six o'clock. Early, as she had guessed; she must have been unconscious for a long time. She listened: absolute silence. It was deathly quiet, no cry from an animal, no call even of a waking bird. Eerie: perhaps it was still snowing, blanketing all sound, but the place seemed deserted. At least there was nobody around for the moment.

She was in a barn, sitting on a heap of scratchy straw. Someone had left an old horse blanket at her feet. She pulled it up around her and breathed in the familiar animal smell: a comforting childhood memory. A bottle of water, a piece of bread and an apple lay in an old tin lid beside her. Well, thought Emma, they wouldn't bother to leave food and a blanket if they were intending to kill me. There would be no point in that, so that's one brightening thought. There was a lofty window, too far out of reach to see much except to the sky – the area of light on which she had first focused. A pair of huge double doors faced her, with a smaller entrance positioned in one side. Emma got up slowly, feeling a little dizzy, leaning against the wood and carefully testing her stiff limbs as she regained her balance. The distance to the doors seemed so far, in her weakened state, but with difficulty she reached them – solid, heavy, thoroughly shut, locked and bolted from the other side. Without doubt, no escape that way.

A defunct ancient tractor stood against the wall opposite the window. It offered, thought Emma, the only possible means of seeing outside. If she climbed onto the seat and stood up she just might be able to get a view and have some idea as to where she was. This could prove fairly precarious and Emma still felt too feeble to try; she'd have to sit, eat and regain her strength a bit first.

She did feel better after eating. Then very cautiously, Emma managed to climb onto the tractor and get a glimpse of the world outside. The sun was up: it glowed pinkly beautiful through the top branches of a snow-laden tree. More positive thinking thought Emma, pleased that she'd achieved this small goal. Judging by the position of the sun she suspected that she was somewhere up on the mountain range opposite the hotel. She could just see the edge of other farm buildings, most likely deserted as they would be too high for winter use. Such farms were closed up at this time of year, until the snows left. There was something vaguely familiar about the weather vane on one of the roofs. Where had she seen one like that before?

Sitting down, huddled in the blanket for warmth, Emma considered her options. A plan of action depended on how many assailants she had. It was nearly daylight, so she reckoned that they were bound to return before long to see if she was still alive and kicking. She couldn't hope to fight off or outwit more than one man. Emma decided the best plan was to feign continued unconsciousness while assessing the situation. First she had to hide the fact that she had both drunk and eaten. Whilst dead to the world she could have turned over and upset the tin, she thought, as she covered the contents with loose straw, contriving to make it look believable. The biggest excitement was that she had found the bar of Swiss milk chocolate, which she'd bought at the airport, still in her pocket. She'd been searching for her mobile, which of course had been removed, but the chocolate remained and had to be the most comforting taste in the world.

Sound suddenly interrupted her solitude; it was just one of the eagle clan, calling to another but punctuated with short bursts of alarm. Then Emma heard an approaching engine. 'Oh God! the monsters are returning. Someone, anyone, please help me!' Panic threatened once more, but immediately she placed her hands across her abdomen willing herself to be calm. 'I must keep my head, for all our sakes. I must think positive and look for a means of escape. How precious life is at this moment of terrifying uncertainty. I must remember to write it all down when I am safe once more, lest I forget.'

The snowmobile had nearly arrived. Emma experienced a fleeting surge of optimism; perhaps it was help come to rescue her. No way. Who could possibly know where she was, except her captors, whoever they were. Returning the blanket to where it had been left, Emma lay, placing her body in such a position as to hide the food tin and water from sight. As she waited in dread, the cold clammy fear made her shiver uncontrollably, clinging to her body like a shroud. She stretched her limbs, while she still could, to keep the circulation going. Then she must keep still. If they thought her unconscious they could do anything with her, but she still thought it the best option and perhaps, she reasoned, they needed to keep her unharmed and in one piece, for bargaining power, as she had nothing else to offer. Her instinct to survive had never been stronger than at this moment with a precious tiny new life to protect.

Emma knew she just had to hang on to the fact that these people didn't want her dead and that soon she'd be tucked up in the hotel with the others. Tears ran down her face stinging the livid patch where she'd been slapped. It made her angry, which gave her strength, but at the same time made her head begin to throb. She'd been moving around too soon and should have stayed still longer. It must have been quite a blow to have produced such a bump and she must also be suffering from shock.

Odd thoughts were washing through her brain as if it was searching for something just out of reach. As the small barn door opened, her heart lurched with fright and then it came to her. Emma knew where she was.

"I'm afraid I have some bad news." announced Guy sitting across the table from Marc in his towelling robe. It was early in the morning and the others weren't up. After the illuminating call from Zak, on his mobile at dawn, he'd managed to leave his room without disturbing Alicia. He'd already been down in the village for several hours.

The ever present doctor in him had enabled Marc to wake at the first gentle knock on his door. He knew in an instant that something had to be seriously wrong to be woken at this hour.

"I'm so sorry about this," Guy continued. Poor man, how was he going to take it he thought, hesitating before launching forth.

"Out with it then," said Marc, an uncomfortable feeling of foreboding settling in. "Is somebody ill?" He made to get up. "I'll get my stuff. I always carry it." Guy stretched out a steadying arm, shaking his head.

"No, no-one's ill, it's not that." Marc settled himself in the chair again and looked squarely across at Guy.

"What is it then? Come on, no sense in beating about the bush, let's have it straight."

"Alright, well... it's Emma actually..."

Marc looked up startled, horrified.

"What? What on earth has happened?"

Guy cut in and said in a rush: "Look she's probably fine, but the fact is that she's been taken and I'm afraid it's all to do with this bloody business here."

"What are you talking about... taken? Emma's in London," replied Marc, tense with apprehension.

"No she's not. That's just it: she wanted to surprise you, she's not in London, she's here and it's all gone belly-up I'm afraid." Guy answered bluntly.

"What do you mean she's here? Of course she's not here; she's coming out at the weekend. I'll ring her at once." Marc, now quite agitated, began again to rise from his chair. Guy put out a restraining arm saying firmly, "No Marc, sit down a minute and please listen to me."

Marc flopped down and then, with an obvious effort, straightened his back and pulled himself together. The well practiced, professional self control took over and he sat quietly listening to what Guy had to tell him.

After Guy had finished filling Marc in with all the details to date, the young doctor sat without speaking, studying his hands for a minute, while the information sank in. 'These hands', he was thinking, 'are used to saving lives; but how the hell they can be of use now to my darling wife, in her present plight, is totally beyond my comprehension'.

Guy sat watching Marc struggling as he came to terms with the situation and admiring the self discipline as it took hold once more.

The doctor looked up, himself again and spread his hands, palms out, in front of him.

"OK, how can I help?"

Guy didn't answer, but smiled at the earnest face in front of him and nodded, knowing for certain that this man could be relied on in a crisis, whatever the future held. Marc continued with his train of thought.

"So, they missed their quarry on the train, the scientist's brother; then obviously made a snap decision to take Emma instead. You think that she's to be used for trade by these people, to reclaim the Iranian scientist, tucked away up the mountain?"

"Yes we think so. Most likely because she was a vulnerable-looking girl, travelling alone and is English. We're waiting to hear," agreed Guy.

"Who exactly are 'we'?" Marc, Guy realized, was both quick and perceptive.

"Myself, Julian and... various others," answered Guy shortly and looking away for an instant.

"I see..." said Marc, "but so far as you can tell she's still alive and unhurt?"

"Yes, pretty sure, other than being knocked out when she was taken. It seems she's alright at present." At this last comment Marc looked up suitably shocked.

"Bloody hell! They knocked Emma out? Why? You said they had guns?"

"Yes, they did and I'm afraid they silenced her because, in spite of the weapons, she obviously gave them quite a run for their money. The train driver said that she was wearing high heeled boots and fair whacked her abductors on the shins as they struggled to get her out of the train. Judging by the yelps of pain, he'd said, Emma managed to inflict some damage before they laid her out. She's a brave girl, but it might have been better for her if she'd just given in and gone quietly."

Marc allowed himself the suggestion of a smile.

"No, she'd never have given in without a fight; that's typical of my wife. You and I both know from previous experience that Emma is extremely courageous and will certainly keep her head, no matter what happens."

"Well then, she's obviously not going to make this easy for them. Rest assured they want the scientist back and they won't dare harm her further whilst negotiating. She's too valuable a bargaining tool."

"Any ideas as to where they are holding her?"

Guy shook his head. "No. Not yet. She could be in France, or possibly Italy, but in fact I think it's more likely she's closer at hand; easier for the exchange. These people are foreigners and, judging by their methods to date, are unsophisticated and unlikely to have a large operation backing them up over here. That would be too conspicuous. I think she's still in these mountains and, if that is so, we will find her. But we do have to be exceedingly careful. You do understand that don't you?"

"Yes," replied Marc, "and I am also well aware that the Swiss and everybody else will wish to keep the scientist here, at all costs... but not at Emma's expense, not if I have anything to do with it."

"Don't worry, we have ways and means of arranging matters, shall I say... a little independently. Now would you mind trying her mobile, just in case she still has it with her, although I'm afraid it's unlikely."

As Marc scrambled to get his phone, a look of hope flittered across his face when he tried Emma's number, but to no avail. It was dead. He'd had a text from her only yesterday afternoon and he had sent her a good-night message. He realized now that she hadn't replied. She hadn't been able to. She was already in the hands of some madman. Marc was devastated to discover this one possible line of communication was now closed. Guy could only imagine how the poor man must be feeling.

"I didn't expect her to answer, but keep trying. Now I'm going out with Julian to organize a few things. I have to see Hélène first. She's the only one who knew of

Emma's altered travelling plans and had expected her to arrive yesterday evening. At dinner time when she hadn't turned up Hélène rang the station. A man who she didn't know merely told her that there had been some problem on the line and so imagined that Emma, amongst others, had spent the night in another hotel somewhere else. All the stranded passengers would have been looked after. The Swiss are very good at seeing to alternative arrangements. So this sounded perfectly acceptable.

"Not realizing that anything was seriously wrong she still didn't want to spoil the surprise for you and so only told me about this late last night. I thought that it was odd that Emma hadn't at least rung Hélène, so I got in touch with my own lines of communication. Alicia luckily was flat out asleep when the information I needed came through on my mobile. There had been an 'incident' and Emma's train had never arrived.

"The train had been shunted into a discreet siding while investigations began. It would have taken them a while to gather up and to interview all the passengers and to discover the identity of the abducted young woman. It's taken me all this time to get clearance to finally get all the details of the situation from the various police authorities here." Guy stood and placed his hand gently on Marc's shoulder, then looking him straight in the eye once more tried to reassure him, saying:

"I'm not in my own country of course but Marc, I promise you, I will do everything in my power to achieve Emma's safe return. I will keep you informed and will call upon your help whenever we need you, but for the moment I want you to try to keep the others calm and occupied, particularly Rose and Oliver, who I suspect see themselves as the leading lights, ready for action. I haven't yet told Alicia of the situation as I wanted to talk to you first. I'll have a word with her too before I go. You are bound to have a visit from the police soon because you are next of kin and they now know that you are here. They will know that I have told you that Emma has gone missing, but that is all. Hélène will be there to help, should you need a translator. I have indicated that you ought to be the one to tell Emma's family if you so wish. I suggest you just answer their questions for the moment, don't voice any other ideas or opinions and certainly don't alert them to the conversation that we have just had. I will talk with their senior officer later. Make no mistake, the shit will hit the fan when the hotel gets to know of your wife's abduction or if someone leaks the story to the press first."

The cold, raw facts brought the hideous nightmare to a reality. The strain was overwhelming but Marc, distressed as he was, knew that he had to hold himself together for everybody's sakes. He ran his hands through his hair while collecting his thoughts, then said quietly:

"Alright. Yes, I understand all that. But can we leave my in-laws out of it, just for the present? I'd rather not have to cope with them, on top of everything else and they would be bound to want to come rushing out here. Luckily they are in India on holiday at the moment and Emma's brother is travelling on business in the USA. They shouldn't get wind of what's happened. So just for twenty-four hours let's keep a lid on it. All I can say to you Guy is thank God you are here, and wish you and Julian the very best possible luck in this appalling mission, with my wife at its centre."

His voice faltered and he looked again at his hands.

"I just wish that I could do something… anything. I feel so utterly helpless."

"Believe you me, I do know how you feel," answered Guy kindly, "but you just have to trust me and keep faith that all will be well in the end. Now I'm sorry but I really must go."

Then he was gone and Marc was left sitting by himself, miserably staring around the poignantly empty room.

✳ ✳ ✳

CHAPTER 12

THEY were bending over her, having an argument. Emma was struggling to keep her breathing laboured, yet relatively normal. She couldn't stop the shivering and wished she could understand something of what the men were saying. Oh God! Now, one was prodding her like a piece of meat and touching her breast; making sure she was really out of it, she imagined.

She moaned and moved into the foetal position, indicating resentment even if she was insensible. When the man began to lift her skirt and feel around her legs, grunting with pleasure, Emma knew her time was up. She was not going to just lie there, no way. She was going to protect her baby from this horror even if she died doing it.

Suddenly there was mad confusion and noise; loud, incessant barking close at hand. The men jumped up in alarm, turning towards the aggressor. Emma chanced a quick look, without raising her head. A large mountain dog was crouched in the doorway, furiously barking its head off. She didn't move but continued to watch; the men weren't sure what to do and they were frightened, obviously unused to animals, thought Emma, fleetingly optimistic. Momentarily they had forgotten her. One of them raised a gun to point at the dog and the other hissed and swore, presumably telling him to put it away, as he immediately lowered his arm. They obviously wouldn't wish to advertise their whereabouts with a bullet and there might, just possibly, be somebody with the dog, or at least within the vicinity.

Emma felt hope flood through her brain, filling her body with renewed energy. The angry dog had been sent from heaven, but she must stay still a little longer. The next few moments were crucial. The huge creature was now crawling along the ground, its head lowered and its eyes fixed on the men as it advanced towards them, snarling with bared teeth. The foreigners were panicking, shouting and bumping into each other, working their way around the edge of the barn towards the entrance. One picked up a log and threw it, missing by far. The dog ignored Emma and, growling, angrier than ever, continued tracking the men who, thoroughly scared now, suddenly made a dive for the doorway. The animal instantly raised its huge bulk off the floor and sprang after them; they leapt out and, just in time, slammed the door in its face. It stood there and howled with frustration.

Emma heard the door being hastily bolted, but waited before sitting up, just in case they were trying to see through a gap in the wooden door. She could hear them outside, arguing in an agitated state then talking on a mobile, as if taking unwelcome instruction. The heated conversation ended abruptly. The dog was still growling on the inside. She listened: silence from the other side of the door, except for the scrunch of boots moving back and forth in the snow. Then with much frustrated-sounding swearing, they were trying to kick-start the snowmobile. At the third attempt it coughed and spluttered into life and soon after they were gone, the laboured engine sounds becoming ever more muffled as, thankfully, they moved away into the distance.

The enormous, bear-sized dog was still whining at the door. Emma sat up and called to it softly. She wasn't afraid; she loved animals and this one was not only beautiful, but also had possibly just saved her from an horrendous fate. Thanks to the dog, for the moment at least, the hideous nightmare had receded.

"Come… here… come here boy. Come on, I know you're a friend."

The lovely mountain dog turned around to look across at Emma then, wagging its tail, ambled over and with a large, slobbering tongue began to lick the streaming tears from her sore face. She in turn merely hugged the huge, comforting, warm body in pure relief.

❇

Emma sat quietly beside the animal, relishing the fact that the men had left and, she felt sure, weren't likely to return for a while. They'd most likely gone for help and further orders. She was safe, for now, but she mustn't waste time. She knew that it was necessary to make a plan.

The young woman felt dishevelled, exhausted and hungry. If only she could be in a hot bath in the hotel, looking forward to lunch with the others; even her trousers were covered in dried mud from climbing up onto the tractor. Emma studied the stains for a minute then looked across at the ancient vehicle which had so willingly supplied the offending dirt. The grooved wheels were ingrained thickly with red clay.

The rich earth didn't look that old. Emma's eyes dropped swiftly to the floor of the barn where there was more discarded debris and two obvious indentations; lines in the straw, between the tractor and the door – wheel marks! Perhaps, just perhaps, this particular piece of farm machinery wasn't quite as dysfunctional as she had at first thought. Laying a reassuring hand on the dog's head she stood up.

"Stay there a minute… good dog," she stroked his ears. "Maybe we can find a way out of here, after all."

The mud, in the thickest places on the huge wheels, was still attached. The tractor had been used relatively recently, certainly in the autumn before the first big freeze. With a surge of excitement, Emma clambered once more up onto the seat and looked in the ignition. Empty: no key.

"Damn, blast and bloody fucking hell…!" she exploded out loud. "Why, oh why couldn't the stupid farmer have left the key here, just this once?"

Despondently, Emma got down again, returning to sit beside her new friend, who was looking somewhat surprised at this last outburst. 'Why would the wretched man take the key away? For heaven's sake, surely no-one would want to pinch a tractor from up here.'

Her eyes scanned the barn for niches or ledges or even a hook, where he might have left it hanging. She got up again and walked around the barn searching, just in case she'd missed a hiding place.

The barn was simply built and other than an empty old manger across one corner, there were no other additions to the inner, wooden walls. Presumably the building was only used for animals in summer and storage in the winter.

She walked over to where there stood a large bucket, a broom and some paint pots. Not yet giving up, Emma considered the collection. 'Now, if it were me where would I hide the key if I did choose to leave it here?'

She lifted each pot in turn, to look underneath. The last was an empty tin with a small full one, set inside. She lifted the little tub and there, miraculously, underneath, lay what could be the elusive key.

Emma snatched it from its hiding place letting out a whoop of triumph. The dog arrived at her side wagging his tail.

"Look," said Emma, holding out the key to show him. "We've got it! We've actually got it! Now, if only I can start the blessed machine and remember my lessons on a smaller version years ago we'll be in with a chance."

First, Emma went again to examine the entrance to the barn and discovered there was plenty of 'give' in the great doors which, although solid, seemed to be only one board thick. Most likely, she thought, they would be secured by one bar, across the middle, on the far side. Good. Now for the tractor!

On the third attempt, after finding and pulling out the choke, the old tractor stuttered reluctantly into life. Emma let it run for a minute and then, using the clutch, she tried out the gear stick and located the brake. The workings appeared relatively simple. She carefully pushed in the choke, thrust the gear into first then let up the clutch too fast and the machine jerked forward and stopped. Not enough acceleration. She swore and tried again; it started first flick and, carefully letting up the clutch, the great machine began to lumber slowly forward.

❋

It was mid-morning. Guy and Julian sat together in a bar down in the town of Spieglesee, discussing the latest information that they had just received from Zak at the top of the mountain.

Emma's abductors had been in touch with the local Cantonal police: her life for those of the Iranian scientist and his brother; just as they had all been expecting. No money was requested, merely a simple exchange and safe passage out of the country, back to Iran. Fedpol was immediately informed and a team coordinated. The newly arrived Foreign Office official from the UK and the scientist's remaining relative, his brother, together with Zak and the two Swiss bodyguards, were now also holed up in the safe house high up the mountain. A representative from Fedpol was on his way.

"Zak says he thinks that nobody will budge, that there will be no deal and no negotiation." Guy, frowning, was contemplating their options.

"No, but with Emma being a British citizen they are bound to stall for time, while they send out a specially trained force to look for her," Julian replied, with very little conviction.

"Yes, but they'll take a while to coordinate an operational force, with local knowledge of these mountains. With any luck our permissions will come through first, which will give us a head start."

"Do you think they'll lend us Zak?"

"I don't see why not, providing he's well replaced up in the house," Guy answered, adding, "I've asked for Oliver as well; I hope you agree with that?"

"Yes, if you're happy and reckon he's up to it?"

"He's fit and strong and has spent quite long periods with the TA. Yes, I think he'd prove to be a help, besides which we haven't got the time to be too choosey. As soon as we get authorization, I want to move, before the whole mountain range is alive with the Swiss Enzian task force. At that time, in my opinion, Emma's chances will be severely reduced. Too much activity in the area and our adversaries may well panic."

"What do we do about the others and Marc?" Julian asked anxiously.

"Marc is no problem and he'll be good with the girls. I'll fill Alicia in with the bare facts and she'll pass on the info to Adriana; they'll be totally discreet. It's only Rose I'm concerned about. She's a determined creature, a bit of a 'dare devil' I suspect. And she feels responsible for setting the ball rolling by finding the blood in the snow in the first place. They may have a job keeping her quiet, but they must all stay out of harm's way, in or around the hotel for the moment. That's of paramount importance."

"Absolutely," agreed Julian, getting out the inevitable cigarette. "They've all been involved more than enough already... God Almighty! How is it that every time we plan a break, it inevitably seems to get mucked up by someone else's horrendous drama?"

"Wrong place, wrong time unfortunately; although as it's turned out it's bloody lucky we are here," Guy said getting up, frowning and adding quietly, "but our friend, the doctor, must be worried sick and just imagine what poor Emma must be going through, wherever she is; although my gut feeling is that she is still somewhere close by. Let's just hope to God that she is still of this world and so far unharmed."

❈   ❈   ❈

CHAPTER 13

ROSE was really becoming quite annoyed with Oliver. Whenever she tried to get him to talk about the recent dramatic events he refused, not exactly outright, but he would just keep changing the subject. Also, she was sure that he knew a lot more about what was presently going on than she did and that really wasn't fair, particularly as she had been the one to have first discovered the evidence of a likely crime.

Actually, all the men seemed to have clammed up and both Alicia and Adriana now appeared less interested as well, almost putting her off each time she raised the subject. All she had been told was that there had been a murder – some row that had got out of hand between some immigrants who'd come into the country illegally and that the authorities were dealing with it. In that case, why on earth was Oliver so reluctant to be drawn any further on the matter? Quite simply, Rose didn't believe the story.

*

When Guy and Julian returned, Marc had decided that he would ask if he himself could tell Rose what had happened to Emma. He could understand perhaps a little of how she must feel now, being kept in the dark when pretty much the whole wretched saga had started when she'd found the blood in the snow to begin with. Besides, it would give him something to do while he waited for news of his beloved Emma. It just didn't bear thinking about what her abductors might do in order to achieve their own ends. Marc couldn't imagine being in a worse predicament. The only thing to latch on to was the fact that, as Guy had told him, it served no purpose at all for the Iranians to harm Emma. Their only interest was in the exchange and repatriation of their own countrymen.

As expected Rose was unashamedly horrified when she heard the news of Emma's abduction. Marc had suggested a short walk before lunch, in order to tell her privately. The other two men were busy in their rooms bringing Alicia and Adriana up to date, after which they were all going to meet for a meal.

Rose stopped dead and stared up at Marc's anguished face in shocked disbelief. She took hold of his arm for support, then opened and shut her mouth, unable, for the moment, to speak. Marc put his arm around her shoulders and waited for her to recover herself. Strong girl, he thought, as he watched her take a visible hold of herself for his benefit. Rose was bright red in the face with emotion and her eyes were full. But she blinked twice, cleared her throat, swallowed and then said stiltedly:

"Right... I understand... God! Marc... I just can't imagine what this ghastly situation must be like for you... I've never heard of anything so horrible... I'm so sorry, it must be a living hell not knowing where Emma is or if she's being well treated, or even if she's... she's alright." She stopped herself abruptly, squeezed his arm for comfort then launched forth again, in a more determined tone. "I am very well aware that both Guy and Julian are muddled up in their own very secret world, but we can't just sit here doing nothing... so what on earth can the rest of us do to help?"

Marc smiled at her, grateful for her thoughtfulness and obvious courage in her immediate wish to become further involved, but this he knew was exactly the situation that Guy most dreaded. Rose crossing the hidden boundaries, setting off to do some investigating on her own, could well put Emma's life, not to mention her own, in further jeopardy. It needed careful and professional handling. They turned together to walk back to the hotel and he changed the direction of the conversation.

"Rose, you really are something. When you two meet you'll get on like a house on fire; Emma will like you very much indeed. In this present very uncertain world, that is one thing that I am one hundred per cent certain about." But Rose wasn't to be put off so easily.

"Um; well yes I'm sure that I'm also going to like Emma very much, but Marc... seriously, we must be able to do something to help, we can't just sit around twiddling our thumbs!" She paused just long enough to catch her breath, then continued conspiratorially in a rush, "I think that Olly is in really deep with Julian and Guy. I'm really worried as they're obviously experts in this field; Olly is not. He has merely done courses and weekend stints with the TA to keep himself fit, because he works all week in an office."

Rose looked up at Marc to judge his reaction: but he looked somewhat unsurprised, almost as if he too knew more than he was letting on. Her eyes flashed.

"Well, if they can't tell us what's going on then I intend to do a little sleuthing myself." Marc tried another tack.

"Rose, you have to promise me two things: first, that you will not go far from the hotel on your own and, secondly, that you will not take any action whatsoever without telling me, as not only could it be dangerous for you, but to all the others as well, not least to Emma herself. Alicia and Adriana are in exactly the same position: they also want to help but realize that there are others out there who, without interference, are far better equipped to achieve Emma's safe return. Do you understand what I am saying?" he finished quite severely.

"Yes, of course," replied Rose deflating and a little ashamed of her thoughtless exuberance. They walked back in silence then Rose tucked her arm through his and said, "I'm sorry Marc," her voice faltered, "really I am... I only want to help bring Emma safely back to you and... in one piece," she finished in a barely audible whisper: "that's all."

"I know," he replied, "and you're sweet and brave... now come on," he said looking up at the sky, "it's going to snow again, so let's find the others, have something to eat and make a plan to do something positive with the rest of the day. It's the only thing we can do." He raised his eyes heavenwards, once more, saying a silent prayer that Emma had thought to travel in her warmest clothes. Her coat hadn't been found on the train, so hopefully she had it on wherever she was.

❋

"Rose is annoyed with us for keeping mum." Adriana and Alicia were sitting together in Alicia's room before lunch. Julian and Guy had gone for a quick swim in the hotel pool with Oliver, or so they'd said.

"I know, but it's best Marc tells her as he's in a horrible situation and she'll have no choice but to listen and do as he asks," replied Alicia. "She might not pay much attention to us."

136

"Yes I agree, but I have to say I too think it's pretty awful having to sit around here, biting our fingernails, waiting for news, particularly as in our case Emma is such a close friend. God Ally! I'm so worried for her. Do you think she's alright?" Adriana took a handkerchief from her jeans pocket and blew her nose loudly. Alicia got up and went across to look out of the window. She was momentarily silent and her eyes had a faraway look when she turned back to Adriana.

"Yes, I do think she's probably alright so far. Emma's intrepid. She's been in tricky scrapes before and come out on top. She won't give up that easily. If there's a way out of wherever she is, then I'm sure Emma will find it. But tell me again: what did you really make of those two men? If they really are responsible for her abduction it would be good to have some idea what we are up against. After all, Ari, you and Marc saw them at very close hand."

"Yes we did and we had quite long enough to make an assessment. I told Guy that if it's the same pair holding Emma, I think she has every chance of out-witting them, if she keeps her head. They are a freaky couple, unprofessional and easily unnerved, I'd say, judging by their performance with the cows. But they have fire-arms and may have extra help at hand by now, wouldn't you think?"

"I don't know," answered Alicia. "Guy also seems to think that they are a fairly unsophisticated lot, so hopefully they'll give up when they realize the Swiss aren't easily persuaded, leave her and flee, worried about their own skins." Adriana looked at her watch and shrugged resignedly.

"Well, let's hope so, but I can't imagine the trouble they'll be in if they arrive back in Iran without their fellow countrymen. Oh well, I suppose we'd better go down and meet the others for lunch."

"Yes. I don't know about you but I'm not the least bit hungry," replied Alicia, getting up "and it will be bloody awkward, especially for Marc, what with the whole world and its mother talking about the kidnapping of his wife."

"Come on then, let's go and do our bit, but we'd better go carefully with Rose."

"Yes, extremely carefully," agreed Adriana. "I really do feel that she is more than capable of taking things into her own hands, especially as Olly now seems so involved with our men."

The two friends locked the room and linking arms went downstairs to face the next instalment in the saga of their frighteningly unusual winter holiday.

✳

Lunch was difficult to say the least. Hélène had discreetly come across with a note for Alicia as they all sat down to wait for the men. Alicia excused herself and went out to read the letter, perfectly well aware of what it might contain. The men would not be joining them as they were about 'other business' which, as she knew, was important. The note read:

'Oliver is with us; try not to worry. Will be in touch when we can. Sustain a low profile, stay close to the hotel and only respond factually to any police questioning. Keep your mobile on (and charged!) and look after each other. At all costs be sure to put a dampener on Rose's enthusiasm. Love to the others and particularly to you and Adriana. G/J and Olly.'

Returning to the table, Alicia merely told the others that the three men were busy elsewhere, but would be back soon. Rose, needless to say, was the first to speak, her face pink with indignation.

"Well, I can't believe that Olly couldn't have said something to me himself before they left; he didn't even say goodbye."

Alicia answered her sensitively, yet firmly.

"No Rose, he couldn't say a thing as he knew what reaction to expect. They were quite right just to go quietly on their way, with no fuss. You must remember this is what Julian and Guy are best at and you should be really proud that they have taken Olly to help them." She looked across at Marc, who caught her eye and nodded in assent. Adriana, smiling brightly to defuse the situation, quickly filled the gap:

"Right then, let's order some lunch and decide what to do this afternoon."

"Good idea," said Marc, handing round the menus. All four people studied the cards, each with their own thoughts kept very much to themselves. Nobody was hungry.

When coffee arrived Rose couldn't bear the atmosphere any longer. She jumped up and in a slightly wobbly voice announced she was going down to the village to buy some shampoo then coming back to the hotel for a snooze.

"If that is alright with everybody else that is?" she finished, looking defiantly across at Alicia.

"But of course. In fact I think that I might follow suit; have a sleep, I mean," answered Alicia tactfully, also standing. "We had a very late night last night. Perhaps we could all do a couple of runs together later, if anybody feels like it." The doctor and Adriana rose from their seats too.

"I think that a rest is a brilliant idea," said Marc quickly, aware of the tense atmosphere. "I've got an excellent book at present, but perhaps, putting on my professional hat for a moment, dare I suggest let's not ski today. The weather's not good and with minds elsewhere, that sort of thing, I really don't want to have to be ministering to those with broken limbs, if you don't mind. Maybe a swim and a sauna later would be a better plan of action." They all managed to laugh and Rose, cheering up, asked if anybody else wanted anything from the local shop.

"No thanks," replied Alicia putting an arm around her shoulders as they walked away from the table. "I don't know about you two, but after all that vin rosé Marc insisted on giving us, I for one just can't wait to get to my bed."

Rose didn't feel at all sleepy or in need of a rest. She went up to her room to get her coat, boots and some money. It was snowing again as she set off down to the village, but she felt much better to be away and out of the hotel for a while. The atmosphere at lunch had been nothing short of claustrophobic. Nobody's fault, but they had all been trying too hard to be cheerful and were, understandably, thoroughly upset about Emma. Also Rose was annoyed with Oliver for having disappeared like that without a word and, much as she had tried, she couldn't hide her indignation from the others. She felt let down.

She thrust her hands deeper into her pockets and bowed her bare head against the swirling snow flakes. After the heat from inside the hotel and the warming red wine at lunch, it felt even colder outside. Marc was extraordinary, considering how he must be feeling. As for Emma: God, what might she be going through; if indeed she was still alive. Nobody had dared suggest anything so horrific, but kidnappings didn't often end happily.

Rose bought the shampoo, hoping that it was in fact shampoo and not conditioner. She couldn't understand the German text on the label and the young girl serving her didn't speak any English. Not yet wishing to return into the rather stultifying warmth of the hotel, Rose decided to drop in at the café by the station. She knew the owner there, so she could also ask about the shampoo.

The heat from inside the café hit her in the face as she walked in. It was always one extreme to the other in this particular climate; hot or cold, thought Rose irritably: nothing in between. As she approached the till Rose realized that the few people, already seated, had all stopped talking and were quite openly observing her. Of course, they would think she was from the hotel and most likely knew the abducted woman as well. It was inevitable as such a dramatic happening, in this peaceful village, was unheard of.

"*Guten Tag* Rose, it's good to see you. Now what would you like on this cold afternoon?" The kind woman was smiling sympathetically.

"Hello Käthi, how are you? May I have a cup of tea please, it's comforting for us English you know." She thought she'd better say no more.

"Of course you can. Coming right up." She leant across the serving table and said gently, "I'm so sorry my dear. *Mein Gott* what a terrible worry for you all." Then she stepped back, indicating with her eyes towards the others in the room. Obviously, as she'd thought, they had all been talking about what had happened to the doctor's poor wife.

Rose went and sat in a corner as far away as possible from anybody else. She cradled her hot tea in her hands, unable to stop her imagination running in the most horrible directions. What if everything goes wrong and I lose Olly as well, she thought, and he never even said goodbye? Surely the three of them wouldn't be involved with anything too dangerous. Their job, she thought, would be merely to help locate Emma. The Swiss special police team would be responsible for the strong-arm stuff. If only she'd been told more perhaps she wouldn't be so worried. The worst thing was not being able to do anything; the waiting was going to prove interminable.

Rose's train of thought was disturbed by a heated argument at the far side of the room; those on two tables were taking part in the discussion. Aware of the disturbance, Käthi, slightly embarrassed, came across to her table to see if Rose wanted anything else to drink.

"No thanks Käthi, but what's the argument about?" Rose asked.

"It's Steffi's mountain dog's gone missing. You know, Steffi who has the farm at the top in the summer. She does meals for the walkers." Emma nodded her head,

"Yes, I know Steffi, she's lovely and I know the farm. It's on the other side. She used to teach people to ski in the winter, didn't she? I remember we had a lesson once."

"Yes, that's her. Well, they are in disagreement as to what has happened to that beautiful dog of hers. Some say it's just gone off wenching and got run over somewhere, or is stuck in a trap. Others say it's been stolen as it's worth a lot of money. I say it's probably gone up to the summer farm thinking it might find some sun. It's not far across the valley." She laughed, perfunctorily wiped the table and went off to see to another customer.

Rose sat thinking. She remembered the beautiful dog from a fleeting summer visit to the mountains a couple of years previously, when she and Olly had been driving out to Italy. She wondered if it had actually gone up to the farm. It would be quite a long way in the snow for a dog, although not so far for people using a newly installed ski lift, pondered Rose, a plan already forming.

How long would it take to get up there? An hour… a couple of hours perhaps in bad weather? She could ski down, albeit off piste. What's more the others would all be asleep and none the wiser. She hadn't actually promised Marc anything and anyway it was on the far side of the valley, away from the hotel and all the action. It would, at least, be something useful to do whilst waiting for news elsewhere.

❄ ❄ ❄

CHAPTER 14

THERE had been many sightings of Emma, even as far afield as Russia. Reports had come in by the dozen. The most likely had been at a remote border between France and Switzerland. The accepted customs post was on a main road a few kilometres away. The minor route, through an isolated farm, was unmanned, considered unimportant and anyway impassable in winter. But it was sometimes used by the younger generation, smuggling in illegal drugs from middle European countries. The farmer thought he'd seen a four-by-four, with a woman answering Emma's description, and two Arab-looking people, pass by just before dark, the last evening. It had turned out merely to be youngsters with a bootload of beer, avoiding the frontier. The Swiss Cantonal police had been given orders to screen diligently all borders, airports and in particular train stations. Emma had apparently been identified on countless occasions, in the company of several Middle-Eastern looking individuals. No stone was to be left unturned to secure the safe release of the young English girl.

Guy and Julian set about their own line of enquiries down in the main town of Spiegelsee, whilst waiting for their operational permits. First they talked to the train driver, a man of about sixty who spoke good English. He had been given a few days off to recover from the ordeal and to help the police in their investigations. He gave a very good description of the two Iranian thugs and of Emma, but was somewhat vague about the other people on the train. Not that it mattered. Guy and Julian were well aware that the scientist's brother, the other asylum seeker, and his escorts would have made themselves scarce once the trouble started. It was quite obvious to them who the assailants had been after.

The ticket inspector, a much older man, was away all day on the Geneva run. The engine driver told them that if it hadn't been for the guns, both he and the inspector would have taken on the foreigners, and the brave little English girl would never have been taken; they could be sure of that. He was still very upset and concerned for Emma and was obviously feeling responsible for not having been able to stop the abduction. "Such violence is unheard of in these mountains," he kept muttering, shaking his head sadly. Guy did his best to reassure the poor man.

The British Embassy in Bern sent through the necessary authorizations, enabling Julian and Guy to proceed with their mission.

Oliver was also given permission to join them, but he was allowed only to carry the small arms that he'd been trained to use with the TA – a Browning 9mm pistol with a spare magazine – and only if deemed absolutely necessary. He was to be used solely as backup and preferably just for the purpose of surveillance. Guy didn't bother to repeat this rather stuffy order as Oliver wouldn't have been at all impressed. He was also told that it was of paramount importance that Zak remained in charge at the top of the mountain. It was considered that he had more than enough to look after. This was a blow as Zak knew the mountains better than anybody.

The three men then headed up the mountain again, to the safe house, to collect the weaponry and supplies they required from Zak. This time Guy wished to meet the senior member of staff who had just arrived to represent the British Ambassador. He wanted to interview the Iranian scientist again, as well as the man's brother, now also installed in the hideaway. An interpreter was already in situ. Guy remained firmly convinced that Emma was being held somewhere within the vicinity. He wanted to accumulate as much information as possible about Emma's likely abductors, before setting out to search for her unobtrusively and hopefully, at least for the moment, unencumbered by the elite Swiss Enzian force. They were presently gathering together their equipment and Alpine expertise. The Alps covered a huge area; a large number of men would be needed in this inclement weather, with plenty of back up from the air. It would take a while to organize; the Swiss wouldn't be hurried, impeccable with their planning.

The Englishmen had journeyed up on the snowmobiles, by way of the hut on the black run, to see if there were any traces of the Iranians left there. Snow was falling thickly, covering their tracks as they progressed, but at the same time wiping out any tell tale signs of the stolen snow machines or any other vital clues. They had already visited the shop which had reported the vehicle theft to the police.

Oliver, although feeling a little guilty to have bailed out without a word to Rose, was in his element. On this occasion he had been allowed to follow Guy and Julian on his own machine. They were all wearing winter weather gear and goggles and it was amazing how warm he felt; mainly, Oliver supposed, because the adrenalin was pumping. He couldn't believe his luck in getting permission to be included in this operation. He could only imagine that his commanding officer in the TA had put in a good word. Oliver had passed out top in the last training exercise which had been spread over a long three-day period, so that must have helped.

Guy also was doing what he was best at, but didn't relish this particular mission, involving someone of whom privately he was so very fond. He was dead worried for Emma and felt a huge responsibility to Marc in setting out to achieve her freedom. But he knew that he must put all negative thoughts out of his head so as to concentrate solely on the job.

Julian always found the emotional side of these undertakings more difficult to put aside. This time it wasn't just about people who were strangers, but a friend who had been taken, and it made him incredibly angry; however he'd also been taught to deal with that anger. He just wished that they'd get more quickly to the hut, so that he could have another cigarette, which always settled him down. That at least was a positive thought for the immediate future.

The higher they advanced up the mountain, the faster the snow seemed to fall, until it became nothing short of a blizzard. The machines struggled on. Oliver couldn't imagine how Guy, in front, could see where he was going. Thanks to the heavy storm they were able to come in close to the hut this time, from the north, and within a matter of minutes their tracks were completely obliterated.

Inside the hideaway it was snug. Zak had the wood-burning stove lit and all the occupants sat around a large wooden table warming themselves before the fire. Zak ushered the newcomers in, bolted the door against the elements, helped them discard and hang up their wet clothes, then turned to introduce everybody.

*

Before leaving the café Rose asked Käthi to make her up a flask of hot chocolate and also bought a packet of sweet biscuits. This was an old lesson learnt from childhood days spent with her grandmother, who never journeyed anywhere without taking something to eat and drink. Whenever someone remarked on her supplies made ready for travelling, she would reply: "My dear, you never know when you, or even somebody else, might need sustenance." Still healthy at ninety she stuck rigidly to this belief.

Rose chuckled to herself as she remembered the old lady's advice and sped back to the hotel. She changed into warm skiwear; left a note on Olly's pillow, just in case he came back first, stuffed everything into her back-pack and went unnoticed down the back stairs to the ski room. There she put on her boots, strapped a pair of the hotel snow shoes to the bag on her back and set off to the station. One stop on the regular little train took her to the next village and to the cable car for the other side of the mountain.

Rose felt excited: wouldn't it be wonderful if she could find the dog for Steffi? Perhaps it really had gone up to its summer home.

Unsurprisingly, there was no queue. Although it was only two-thirty in the afternoon, the snow was putting everybody off. There were never many people out at the beginning of the week anyway. Rose showed her ski pass and asked for an update on the weather.

"*Guten Tag*, I'm afraid it's closing in a bit up there, Miss. Be careful and keep to the pistes, they are well marked."

"Yes, I will, don't worry, thank you, *danke*," answered Rose politely. "Please could I have another map?" He handed it over, proudly pointing out the new lift which had just opened. None of Rose's new friends had skied on this side of the valley this year and the new chair lift appeared to be just what she needed to get her over towards Steffi's property. From the farm, although there was no actual piste, Rose thought that she'd find her way down alright, if she managed to recognize the lie of the land well enough from previous summer walks.

Rose sat alone in the cable car cabin, pleased to be taking some sort of action at last. She wondered what the men were doing and where they were: busy with the police, she imagined. She looked up at the sky. As long as the weather didn't close in completely she'd be back at the hotel long before the others even discovered her missing.

✳

Emma was having difficulty handling the huge tractor. The trouble was that, in the dim light, she hadn't realized that the piece of machinery immediately behind the tractor in the barn was still attached. The implement looked like a small plough or something and she had no idea how to disengage it; so the only thing to do was to try to force the doors again with a bit more speed, dragging the piece of machinery behind. At least it appeared to be raised a bit above the ground. She found a dirty old cushion on the floor of the cabin and placed it on her knees to protect her lower stomach. Then she thrust the gear into first, pushed the throttle fully and let the clutch up with her foot. The vast vehicle leapt forward and Emma, gritting her teeth, braced herself, as this time it hit the wood with full force and she was thrown violently backwards. She clung on to the steering wheel for dear life.

As the heavy tractor hit them, the doors bowed and strained then, miracle of all miracles, the wood began to splinter. The sound of the tearing timber, added to the noise of the revving tractor, filled the barn with fury.

Emma looked back quickly, over her shoulder, to see how the dog was faring. But he was sitting in the corner, patiently waiting and reasonably unperturbed; almost as if this was an everyday occurrence. Then the bar on the far side suddenly gave and the tractor burst out of the barn. She jammed on the brake and slumped forward, almost winding herself. She flung the protective cushion into the back.

Escape! Emma sat up and, unable to suppress a shout of triumph, punched the air. She had escaped.

It was snowing heavily, the sky leaden, but Emma recognised where she was. She was on the far side of the valley from the hotel and this barn was somewhere immediately below Steffi's summer farm. She thought she remembered walking down a hard core track linking the two complexes. It was some distance but, if in the deep snow she could manage to keep on the hard surface, she might make it up there. She could hide the tractor behind a barn and her escape route would be hidden under several inches of snowfall. She checked her watch. Only half an hour had elapsed since the men had left, but she had better get cracking.

Emma climbed down and re-entered the barn, tore the very Scottish collar tag off her shirt and looped it around the bottle top, grabbed the blanket which she wrapped around her unsuitable clothes and called to the dog. He was now standing at the entrance looking somewhat confused. The weather was worsening and it was going to be difficult to see. She picked up a broken piece of wood and made a ramp. The big animal scrambled up into the tractor cabin, surprisingly nimble for his great bulk, where he settled himself more comfortably on an old sack behind the driver's seat.

"Good, you've done this before, haven't you?" Emma decided this was another small goal achieved. Her heart was hammering with excitement and no longer was she aware of her aching head and sore face. She paused a moment placing her hands protectively across her stomach. Could she really outwit these terrible people? And, in doing so, could she manage to hold on to this much longed-for baby? If only she could make it up the mountain as far as Steffi's house, she reckoned that she was in with a chance, on both counts, just as long as the terrible people didn't come back up too soon. "Now where the hell are the windscreen wipers and will they actually work?"

They did. Emma looked behind her once; the snow storm had already partially covered the disturbed ground. It wouldn't take long to conceal the rest and, Emma thought, her inhuman captors were bound to expect her to have set off downhill towards the village. She jammed the gear into first, let up the clutch and the huge machine edged slowly forward up the mountain track.

✳

Guy had all the information he needed and he now had a good idea of the type of people they were up against. Emma's bag had been left outside the police station, in the main town in the valley, with a note. Her luggage, left behind on the train, had been delivered to the hotel by the station master. Her abductors were using her mobile to make contact with each other, which in turn was easier to trace, as all messaging was routed back through the UK. The Iranians were moving around, but as Guy had thought they remained within the vicinity. The Cantonal police were expecting a call from that mobile number at nine oclock in the morning of the following day. Emma's kidnappers were expected to demand a time for the exchange, followed immediately with safe conduct out of the country for the whole party.

Guy checked his watch. They had eighteen hours and about four hours of daylight left now. He hoped it was enough. The special purpose Enzian force was waiting on the result of the phone call in the morning, before going in.

The three Englishmen finished their meeting in the hut and took their leave. They donned their compulsory flak jackets, their outside clothes and stowed the rest of their equipment on the snowmobiles.

Zak was disappointed not to be going with them, yet he well understood that it was all important for him to remain responsible for the scientist's welfare up in the safe house. He wished his friends well and watched them disappear into the murk: the snow was now falling fast and furiously and there was a vicious wind. The departing men were soon invisible and the engine noise muffled to a gentle drone.

'They certainly have the weather on their side in order to go discreetly about their business,' thought Zak, standing alone in the cold, wishing again that he had been in the spare seat on the second vehicle.

❄ ❄ ❄

CHAPTER 15

THE weather had deteriorated badly. Rose stood at the top of the new chair lift, deliberating whether or not to set off in the direction of Steffi's farm. The route down the pisted slope was reasonable and she could see the first three markers; the other uncharted way was quite another matter. If only the cloud would lift for a few minutes, just long enough to get her across this immediate mountain, then she'd be alright: she hoped she'd recognize where she was. She really couldn't give up having got this far. Unsurprisingly, there were no other skiers in sight.

Olly would be absolutely furious with her for setting out on this little jaunt. Rose could just imagine what he'd say. 'I can't believe you could be so stupid to go out in such weather. You must be out of your mind; totally irresponsible; you should know better…' etc etc. Too bad, thought Rose, he shouldn't have gone off without telling me anything about what he was up to with Julian and Guy and anyway… it's not as if we are even engaged or anything. He can't tell me what to do, I am my own person and it's certainly turning out to be some romantic holiday.

She looked up again. There was a glimmer of brightness and it wasn't snowing quite so heavily, just for the moment: time to go, 'onwards ever onwards'. Who was it who had said that – somebody famous? She couldn't remember. Rose set off parallel across the mountain, an accomplished skier even in difficult conditions such as these.

Far below, the lifts were shutting early. The piste runner was the last one to ascend. Not a sign of anyone; sensibly everybody's stayed at home, he thought, pleased and looking forward to a hot shower himself. He set off speedily down the normal ski-run, checking it was empty, wondering if he'd catch up with the pretty young English girl. He thought it unlikely as she looked the part. He imagined she was an expert skier and already enjoying an apres ski drink with her boyfriend, in the warm bar at the bottom. A girl like that was sure to have a boyfriend: odd though, he pondered, that she was out in these conditions and skiing alone. Perhaps there'd been a row.

*

Guy, Julian and Oliver had gone down to Montreux, following a lead. Three unusually shifty-looking people had been meeting most evenings in a restaurant just off the main high street. Last night, outside the back exit, a member of staff had noticed one of the men handing over what looked like a British passport. It was open at the photo of a pretty young woman. The waitress was half English and she recognized the document. One of the other two men snatched the passport, closing it swiftly, as she walked by. The girl thought the incident to be thoroughly suspicious and returned to the restaurant through the main entrance to tell her manager. He, quite rightly, had rung the police who were now awaiting instruction after passing on the information to their senior officers in Bern.

Emma's family had still not been informed of the situation, at Marc's request, as they weren't expected back from India for another week. For the time being Alex, her brother, also remained away from home, travelling on business in the USA. He adored his sister and was also close to Marc. He would have come immediately to support his brother-in-law but Marc, living in hope, was determined to give it just a little longer.

Guy, with his hair plastered over his forehead and in rough work clothes, inspected the other two.

"You'll do," he said chuckling with amusement. Oliver had entered into the spirit of things and really looked the part of a Swiss farm labourer. But Julian, as usual, was fed up with not being allowed to smoke in the restaurant and with not being seen as himself to the outside world. He loathed any form of disguise. Guy leant across the table to address the other two quietly.

"Alright now, are you both clear what I want you to do?" They nodded. Oliver's eyes were bright with excitement. Guy continued.

"I have a temporary waiter, who understands Farsi, ready to look after these people when they come in; should they come in. If we consider them suspicious when they leave, I don't want them out of our sight. If they split up, no problem, one each. Oliver, as I have already said, you are not to take any chance whatsoever. Don't get too close even if he does give you the slip. As we know, they have guns but I suspect are probably more at home with the silence of a knife. So please be aware." Oliver looked as if he had no intention of letting anybody give him the slip. Guy went on, "It's unlikely that we'll loose all three. Once I'm sure they're the ones we're after, the extra help I have lined up will materialize. As long as the Iranians stay together long enough it shouldn't be too difficult. But for the moment, I want them discreetly followed as I believe that, if we are patient, two of them will lead us to Emma. They are, most likely, the two who took her off the train."

"What about getting Marc or Adriana over here, to have a look at these people, in disguise of course? They may well be the pair our friends encountered up the mountain."

"Yes, if necessary we'll do that next; not Marc though. I think it's best if he stays put, at the hotel with the girls: for him, poor man, it's too emotive a situation. Adriana on the other hand... how would you feel about that Julian?"

"Alright... I suppose, as long as she was unrecognizable. She'd be game I'm sure."

"Shouldn't I have a gun as well," Oliver asked hopefully, "just in case."

"No, not at the moment, perhaps later on, depending on the circumstances," Guy answered with a non-committal shake of his head.

"Now remember, if they come in and sit anywhere near, they must not hear any English spoken, only French, or preferably German."

"I'm afraid my German's not up to much, but I can manage a few words." Oliver commented keenly.

"It doesn't matter. We will be listening and not talking much anyway," Julian chipped in, rather curbing Oliver's enthusiasm.

The special waiter approached their table to see what they wanted to drink. All three chose a light beer, which was duly brought. Just before the man returned again to the bar, Guy reminded him to see if he could get a look at any mobiles, describing the phone belonging to Emma in particular.

Half an hour later Guy saw the same waiter speaking intently to one of the girls behind the bar. She was indicating that there were newcomers to be served in a far corner by the door and that he should look after them. The man passed by their table touching Julian's shoulder as he did so. Oliver was the only one facing in the right direction and his eyes were nearly popping out of his head. Guy, with his back to the door, spoke quickly.

"Alright Oliver tell us quickly what you see." Oliver couldn't get it out fast enough.

"Three Indo European-looking people, two fairly scruffy that I've never seen before, but the third..." and it came out in a rush, "is the man I saw, in the hotel, on the first night I was here and what's more he's wearing the same grey duffle-coat which previously caught my attention. Both he and the defectors must have all bought them from the same place when they first came into the country. I wonder if that was pure coincidence or just to add confusion?"

"Most likely chance I should think: probably left in a hurry, and these people would feel the cold here in the mountains. Okay, look away now and drink up, the waiter will do the rest." The young man helping did a good job. He appeared to take some time trying to understand the Iranians' order and then he served several other people before returning to the Englishmen's table. He leant over, near to Guy, as he wiped the table and began to collect up their empty glasses. He talked quickly and quietly, making a certain amount of noise with the tray and glasses as he did so.

"They're speaking Farsi and are discussing going back up the mountain with some food but remaining in the valley, in some guest house, overnight. Also there was some heated discussion about a dog causing a problem. There are a pair of car keys on the table, a Mercedes I think, and the man with the grey coat has a mobile, of the blue colour you described, in his open pocket."

The waiter stood up straight and asked in German if they required anything else. All three declined. Guy took out his wallet to pay. The man bent to receive the money thanking them and adding quietly that he didn't expect the three Persian people would be staying much longer either. They didn't seem settled. Guy and Julian thanked him in perfect German and the man moved away.

"Alright," said Guy as if he was merely continuing a conversation, "they obviously have wheels, so Julian and I will follow the car back to our valley. You Oliver, I'd like to keep an eye on the third member's movements here, if you can, unless he joins the other two. If he does go with the car you obviously come back with us. OK... understood?" Oliver nodded his head importantly. "But," finished Guy, "remember what I said, be careful and keep reporting back. Now we'll go out and have a discreet look around for the Mercedes."

They found the likely vehicle parked half up on the pavement, across the entrance to a building site, on the far side of the street. Their own four-by-four was just around the corner.

*

Rose stood, waiting for the storm to abate, trying to get her bearings before setting off again downhill through the virgin snow, in the direction of Steffi's farm. She knew she had to be well above it. From where she was standing, she thought there was a track going down between the trees. As yet, she couldn't see. The weather was far worse than she expected, but periodically it seemed to lift, just long enough for her to gauge the next part of her route. This was becoming one scary adventure, but she wasn't seriously worried. She was a good skier and knew near enough where she was. Besides which she had a purpose. Rose stared ahead through her binoculars into a silent, grey world, attempting to differentiate between the land and the sky. You could almost imagine anything out there. Snow blindness must be a thoroughly unpleasant experience, she thought, but hang on: wasn't that a pile of logs appearing out of the gloom? In which case she wasn't imagining the way down, there had to be a track for the timber lorries in summer.

Rose was almost where she had intended to be. Without more ado she pointed her skis downhill and, cleaving a remarkably skilled, zigzag pattern through the pure blanket of whiteness, continued once more on her way.

Ten minutes later, lower down the mountain and beneath the dense cloud, the route became easier again. But it was something else in the eerily quiet winter wonderland which persuaded Rose into stopping. The muffled noise of a rough engine was approaching from somewhere below, slicing through the soft, white silence. Who on earth else would be out in this weather, in this closed-off area of the mountain?

Now Rose could see the tops of Steffi's buildings. The distinctive weather vane, on the big barn, stood out starkly. She was nearly there. She had to keep the speed up to achieve the bluff above the farm. From there she could see down into the yard and identify the weird engine noise. She stopped in a triumphant, graceful swirl, which threw up a spray of snow beside her. She'd made it and in near blizzard conditions.

Catching her breath and grinning to herself with satisfaction, Rose listened. The throaty engine noise was louder. Whatever the vehicle, or its business, it would shortly arrive. Some second sense made Rose duck behind a tree. This was no ordinary farm business she felt. Steffi would never send anybody out in this weather: no way.

Out of the murk lumbered the instigator of the noise. Was it a tank or was it a farm machine? Rose, partially hidden from sight, strained her eyes to see. It bumped and strained as the driver endeavoured to line it up at the entrance to the big barn. Peering again through the binoculars Rose couldn't make out the shape of the driver as he appeared to be swathed in a blanket. He was driving an ancient old tractor which was pulling what looked like a small plough. A plough! In this weather – what on earth?

Rose watched, fascinated. The vehicle ground to a halt and the operator was now slumped over the wheel. Rose was just about to move out from behind her tree when the tractor cabin door was thrown open and the man carefully descended, followed by a huge dog. A mountain dog: Steffi's dog. What the hell was going on here? Now he was opening up the big barn door, with some difficulty. It must be very heavy, especially with the snow piling up outside. Then he climbed back up onto the tractor and, clonking the entrance support severely with the plough, managed with a lot of engine revving to manoeuvre the great machine inside. He wasn't a good driver or certainly wasn't used to farm machinery. How odd. Then he came back outside with the dog, shut the door and leant up against it as if exhausted, cradling his stomach with his arms. Perhaps he was ill.

Rose remained riveted, to see what happened next. The extraordinary apparition then dropped to the ground and hugged the dog. The covering blanket fell off and revealed not a farm labourer or a boy, but a woman and in the most inappropriate clothes. The dark-haired girl levered herself upright again and standing stock still looked back the way she'd come, obviously listening. Then, pulling the blanket up around her slight body and calling the dog to her side, she began to trudge wearily, in her unsuitable footwear, up towards the house.

Excitement washed through Rose like a bolt of warm, radiant sunlight, filling her with a relief beyond anything she'd ever felt before. Without any doubt whatsoever, Rose knew exactly who the young woman was. It was Emma. She was alive and Rose had found her.

❊　❊　❊

CHAPTER 16

THE Englishmen sat in the jeep waiting for the call. Nobody spoke. Each was busy with his own thoughts. Oliver was thinking that perhaps he'd rather all the Iranians got into the car together. He didn't really want to be left on his own, following the third man around a strange German-speaking city. He'd prefer to stick with Julian and Guy.

Guy was considering ringing Marc with the news that, as Emma's abductors had been heard discussing taking more food up the mountain, it was likely that she remained unhurt. But perhaps, at this state of play, he shouldn't raise the doctor's hopes too much.

Julian thought their adversaries to be a pretty pathetic looking bunch. Unsophisticated in their thinking and unlikely to be a real threat in action, he guessed. But from his experience, people such as they lost their cool all too easily and in desperation could become reckless. They would need careful handling while Emma was in the firing line. He wished he could get out for another cigarette. Guy wouldn't let him smoke in the car. Guy's mobile rang. He listened then turned to the others.

"OK they're out and heading for the car."

"Together?" asked Oliver hopefully. Guy continued to communicate with the waiter on the other end of the phone while Julian started the engine.

"For the moment... yes... and it looks like they are all getting in, wait... wait... yes they are. Alright we're off. Thank you Andreas, that was brilliant, very well done."

The battered old Mercedes was easy to follow. The man in the duffle coat was driving. They headed out of the town and onto the motorway going in the direction of Italy and the mountains. Julian dropped back several cars when they turned off the main highway to begin the mountain ascent. There was plenty of local rush hour traffic and it was easy to remain incognito. One hour later the little entourage arrived in the home valley. The Iranians stopped at a pizza house in Spiegelsee, the main town. One of the men got out, returning a few minutes later with four large boxes.

"It looks like Emma might be going to get some supper." Julian commented drily.

"Yes it does, but the driver's also getting out... right Oliver you're on. Suss out where the man goes and report back. Remain somewhere across the street and watch for any further movement. Remember what I said: be careful. This man is the boss: he issues the orders to the other two who, I feel sure, are responsible for holding Emma. As I said, don't take any chances, trust your instincts but don't be impulsive and at all times keep in touch. I don't want a dead hero and neither does your girlfriend: understood?"

Oliver nodded and got out of the car trying hard to contain his eagerness.

"Here... take this: but don't use it unless you really have to." Oliver took the gun, checked it was unloaded and stashed it away with the spare magazine in his pocket. His eyes were alight with excitement.

"Thanks, don't worry... see you later." He went off silently, disappearing around the corner after the man in grey.

Julian waited for the Mercedes to move off then allowed two cars and a van to pass by before discreetly following.

*

"Where is Rose?" asked Alicia as they sat beside the fire in the hotel bar. It was early evening.

"I don't know. Perhaps she's still asleep," answered Adriana, "I'll go to see." She got up. "Will you get me another drink please while I'm gone?" She moved off towards the stairs.

"Yes of course," Marc called after her, then turning to Alicia, "I'll order, then whip down to the pool area to make sure she's not gone to sleep in the sauna."

"I have to say I'm a bit apprehensive; she was in a funny mood."

"I know she was, but quite honestly we are all in a strange situation of limbo. I don't expect she's gone far afield."

"I wouldn't bet on it," Alicia mumbled, as Marc went to find the waiter.

A few minutes later Adriana came running down the stairs, in an agitated state.

"She's not there Ally. She's gone out. There's no question about it. The maid let me in and her ski clothes aren't there." Marc had returned, Adriana was upset and in a fluster but with good reason.

"Bloody hell! Where on earth has she gone? Haven't I got enough on my plate? I told her to stay put and not to do anything stupid."

"Shit, shit and shit again, now we have to look for Rose as well. I just can't believe this. You poor man Marc, this really doesn't help, does it?" Alicia exclaimed in a fury.

"Hang on a minute; are you sure she didn't leave a note or something; check the room again Adriana and I'll go and ask at the desk?" Marc experienced another wave of foreboding. He should have known that Rose had no intention of spending the afternoon in bed without Olly.

"I'll go down to the ski room and look there, then I suppose we could go and see Käthi in the café, in case she went there after leaving the shop, which will be closed by now." Alicia glanced at her watch. "If nothing comes to light there I vote we go and check out the bars in Spiegelsee."

"Good idea, but don't let's panic yet: we'll meet back here in a few minutes."

Adriana looked carefully on the dressing table and around Rose's room then she spied the note left on the pillow. Success: she grabbed it up to read, oblivious to the obvious private content.

'Darling Olly, just in case you get back first... have gone to see a man about a dog! Will explain later. Hope you're alright, but can't believe you went without saying goodbye. I love you anyway R' and there was a little drawing of a rose. Quite sweet, but only if under ordinary circumstances, thought Adriana huffily.

'A man about a dog'... what on earth does that mean? She said she was going to buy shampoo. Adriana thanked the maid, who was standing by the bathroom door, waiting patiently to turn down the covers on the bed and left to rejoin the others downstairs.

Marc and Adriana stood in front of the fire with Hélène while they waited for Alicia. They watched her approach. She had a set look on a face masked in anxiety. Marc showed her the note.

"What dog?" She held the note in front of her. "I don't understand, what could she mean? This doesn't exactly help much, does it?" Alicia looked up, "I'm afraid her skis and boots have gone also. Oddly enough, a pair of the hotel snow shoes is missing too and nobody else in the hotel would be stupid enough to take them out in this weather." Hélène sensed the atmosphere of growing alarm.

"I think, if you all agree, that as the weather is so bad I should alert the people who check the pistes at the end of the day and see if any of them remember seeing her. They may well have closed early and she's merely got stuck somewhere. What do you think?"

"Yes, there's no harm in that anyway. Thank you Hélène. We'll go and search out the obvious haunts around here. Let's just hope that she's safe down off the slopes somewhere, cosy and warm and getting plastered."

Hélène went to telephone from the reception desk and the others went to collect their out-door clothes.

"I have a bad feeling about this," said Alicia as she and Adriana went upstairs together.

"So do I. Rose was really pissed off with us all at lunch time. She might well have decided to get away and go skiing by herself."

"You're right and she's a very accomplished skier but she knows the rules. She would never have intentionally stayed out so late. Something else must have happened."

"Yes, that's just what's worrying me," replied Adriana gloomily. "The possibility of that 'something else' – as yet undetermined."

✳ ✳ ✳

CHAPTER 17

EMMA trudged around the back of the house. A wind had got up, she was beginning to feel really cold now and her head was aching badly again. It was almost dark. She had to get inside. Looking behind her the snow was drifting, swiftly obliterating even her most recent footprints. They would never find her now. She was safe.

She wondered if Steffi kept a key anywhere in the vicinity or if she'd have to break a window to get in. The door was obviously firmly locked. She looked round for the dog: where was he? He was sitting underneath the nearest window ledge whining. He was probably hungry also, after their unusual adventure together. He barked at her as if to say hurry up, enough is enough.

"Alright, come on then, let's find the easiest window to force." Emma was beginning to feel nauseous and dizzy again. All the effort, she thought, after the whack on the head and probably the baby too. It would be good to lie down. All the euphoria, after having escaped, was beginning to wear off now and she no longer felt hungry or thirsty. She felt drained both mentally and physically. She just wanted to be warm and to sleep.

She looked around for something with which to smash the window. There were three bricks half covered in snow, underneath the ledge and beside where the dog was sitting. He was looking at her with one paw raised. Brushing off the snow she picked up the top stone and there, in a little hollow underneath, was the key. Emma stared at the dog in astonishment.

"You knew it was there, didn't you? What a clever dog you are." She leant down to pat him once more. Oh dear, she really did feel a bit odd as she staggered back to the door leaning against it for support.

The key turned easily in the well-oiled lock. Emma, followed by the dog, walked in. Relief: another wave of dizziness washed over her. There was a sofa against the far wall, if she could just sit down. The dog began to bark incessantly behind her, as if there was somebody out there. It was unnerving and she wished he'd stop. Emma reached out to a chair to steady herself, before the next wave hit. As her legs began to crumple, her last thoughts were that she mustn't fall: she had to get down quickly and carefully to the rug on the floor, before she passed out.

✳

For the second time that day, Emma regained consciousness. This time her first thoughts were: 'I am comfortable, I am warm, but where am I?' She opened her eyes to look around and remembered. Steffi's house: to which she had escaped. She sensed movement just outside her line of vision. She peered over the edge of the sofa. The lovely dog was lying fast asleep beside her, twitching as he dreamt. The fire was lit. Her wet clothes were in a heap on the floor and she was covered in a blanket with a cushion under her head, but who…?

"Hello, good you're awake." The soft voice came from somewhere behind her. She felt so tired she couldn't have run even if she'd wanted to. Her legs wouldn't have worked. But she wasn't frightened any more. The person with the gentle intonation arrived in front of her and dropped to their knees to stroke the dog. The dog was tranquil. Good sign thought Emma, and the person was speaking English; even better. She raised her eyes expectantly. The pretty, dark girl with the kind, sparkling eyes began to speak slowly and articulately. So I can understand, presumed Emma. She must think me completely out of it.

"Emma, you don't know me, but I'm staying at the hotel with the others. You're safe now. We're in Steffi's house. My name is Rose. It's a long story and we'll talk when you're up to it. You are so brave; I can't get over the extraordinary way you managed to escape. But I think that you should stay still for a bit longer. Go back to sleep now, while I get us something to eat. You have had a very nasty bash on the head and, I'm sure, one hell of a time since you set off from the UK yesterday."

Something to eat. Emma's eyes began to focus on the source of the voice. A twinge in her stomach reminded her that she was now extremely hungry and very thirsty too. The dog had awoken and was staring up at her, panting slightly from the heat of the fire. She brought her hand up from underneath the blanket to stroke his head.

"Yes," she said in a croak. "Actually we are both really hungry, but this beautiful dog has probably just saved my life, so he must have something first." Rose held her gaze and then stretched out her arms as Emma's eyes filled with tears and the flood gates opened.

※

The Mercedes stopped in the little village at the station and pulled into the almost deserted car park which also serviced the skiers' cable car. Guy and Julian had been planning to bring the girls here as there was a good restaurant, well worth a visit, half-way up the mountain.

Now they waited in the road across the street, parked close against the pavement, so as to give other road users a wide berth in these difficult conditions.

"They're sitting in the car, eating their supper," pronounced Julian putting the binoculars down. "Those pizzas are substantial. I know because I had one soon after we arrived. They'll be here for a while so I am going to get out and have a cigarette."

"Alright, I'll ring Oliver while we wait. I'm surprised they have stopped here though."

"Unless they have her somewhere up on this side of the valley," remarked Julian getting out.

"I suppose it's possible, but except for the small ski area, it's deserted up there where we walk in the summer. Nobody lives high up in these mountains at this time of the year. There's no hotel needing supplies and no maintenance cabins necessary. They go up from the bottom to check the lift and piste at night." Julian had shut the car door and was leaning against it. Yes, Guy said to himself, I suppose it is possible that Emma is up there and for that very reason; because it is deserted.

Guy reckoned that Oliver was in a slightly agitated state. His surveillance job was proving difficult. The duffle-coated man had gone into a guest house, but only stayed there long enough to eat the pizza. According to Oliver he'd come out again, and ever since he'd been walking around smoking, deep in thought, quite obviously distracted and making endless calls on his mobile. Oliver thought that he'd been noticed.

"Alright, where are you as regards the station?"

"Very near. The guest house is just across the street. He's been going around the block and came into this café once, to buy a takeaway coffee. That's when I think he might have recognized me."

"Right... we're in the next village, get on the train and come here. They run frequently for the skiers; about every half hour or so at this time of the evening. I think that it's quite probable they have Emma up the mountain on this side of the valley. We are waiting while these two demolish their supper, in their car. It's a tiny village. If we're still here you'll find us parked outside an antique shop, in the street leading away from the car park, opposite the station's main entrance. Keep your head down and skirt the car park circumference. If we are not here it means they've moved on and we've followed. In that case, wait at the station until further notice."

"OK, I'm on my way."

Julian got back in the car.

"I think they are on the move again. Keep well back though, they'll have trouble skidding in that old Merc. As yet the snow plough hasn't been along here."

The Mercedes slid back onto the road and continued somewhat unsteadily out of the village for about two kilometres, where it turned off up a track and with difficulty disappeared behind an unlit, deserted barn. Guy drove on past, together with a motor bike and a large white van; then pulled in and stopped, dousing the lights. They got out and listened. They could hear the muffled noise of a smaller engine sputtering to life behind the building and could see a pale wash of light. Julian and Guy turned to each other thankfully.

"They have a bloody ski-mobile. This is the place and they're going up."

"Good," answered Guy. "Let's get back to the station and collect Oliver, then organize some machines for ourselves. Zak has relations down here who are farmers. They'll have one. Call him while I drive."

As they drove back past the barn they stopped again to look and listen. They could see a pinprick of light and hear the noise of the snowmobile floundering in the deep snow, becoming ever more distant as it began its arduous ascent up the mountain.

"The snow has eased off a bit, but it's drifting in the wind," Julian said. "Nonetheless, we shouldn't have trouble picking up a recent trail if we're quick. I expect they'll be gone a while; that machine didn't sound in particularly good nick."

"No it didn't, which might buy us more time. We'll also arrange a welcome party, for when they return to the car. We'll demobilize it just in case they give us the slip up there. We might leave Olly to organize that. Right, let's get going now. I want to get up there after them as soon as possible." Guy thrust the four-by-four into gear and it lurched forward strongly and solidly on the slippery road surface. Julian took out his mobile to ring Zak.

*

Alicia led the small party into Käthi's bistro. It was cold and dark outside and the café was warm and welcoming, although a little too brightly lit for some tastes. Käthi looked pleased to see them. She liked to think that she catered for everybody and she knew full well that her strudel was better than most. The hotel sent her plenty of custom and she now had a good handle on the basics of most European languages. But she judged that, on this occasion, this particular party of English were not coming in to socialize or to sample her cooking. They appeared worried and she felt immediate sympathy for them all up at the hotel. What with that poor girl being taken, it didn't bear thinking about what might have happened to her. Nowhere was safe anymore it seemed.

"Hello, Käthi, *Wie geht's dir?* How are you?" called Alicia, endeavouring to be cheerful as they walked in. Their hostess smiled in answer to Alicia's good attempt in German.

"*Hello liebling, Guten Tag,* to you all, *kann ich lhnen helfen,* how can I help you?" she asked, holding her hands out to them in greeting.

"Käthi! Have you by any chance seen Rose? We made a sort of plan to meet up. We think that we misunderstood and that perhaps she's gone off somewhere else, to look for us." She finished in a rush. Käthi wasn't taken in. She could see just how anxious they all were. Not surprising, she thought, if a second person also went missing, given what had already happened.

"*Ja, ja,* Miss Rose has been in here. I made up a flask of *heisse schokolade* for her and she took some *güetzi.*" The others all looked astonished.

"Hot chocolate and biscuits?" echoed Marc. "But what on earth did she need them for?"

"Certainly not to eat in her room," muttered Adriana.

"*Natürlich,*" said Käthi. "I did think it odd that she was intending to set out somewhere in this weather and by herself."

"But where was she going?" interrupted Adriana.

"I really don't know... unless... *nein... sicher nicht,* no surely not." She looked up, almost uncomfortable for a second.

"What is it Käthi? Think... it's really important if you can remember anything that might help us find her." Alicia was beginning to sound a little desperate. The poor *liebling,* thought Käthi.

"Well, it was about Steffi's dog going missing... *ja* she seemed very upset."

"Steffi's dog... wait a minute... Marc have you still got her note?" They got out the scrap of paper to scan it again. Then Alicia blurted out.

"Oh Käthi, you don't honestly think that she went looking for the dog do you... and in all this snow?"

"*Nein, nein...* although there was some discussion in here earlier as to what had happened to it. I said that I thought the old dog might have gone up to the summer farm, to see if he could find the sun!" she chuckled, the others all gaped and were speechless as this information sunk in. Marc was the first to recover.

"My God, perhaps she did go up the other side and took the new lift on."

"And that's what she meant in the note, about going to see a man about a dog." Alicia continued.

"Yes," Adriana chipped in, "but the new chair lift is nowhere near Steffi's farm, surely. Or is it?"

"I don't know. None of us has used that one yet, but I think that you might be able to get across from it."

"I think we need a map of that area," Marc cut in. "Let's go back to the hotel. They'll also have Steffi's winter house telephone number down in the valley."

Well, thought Käthi as they all thanked her and left her little haven. What extraordinary goings on and all because of a dog. There never was a dull moment running her café and she just loved being at the hub of it all.

❉ ❉ ❉

CHAPTER 18

EMMA sat up, cradling the mug of chocolate in her hands and, in between sips, munched on a biscuit. Nothing had ever tasted so good. Rose had found some tins of dog food and the big animal was tucking in greedily beside her. Emma turned her head to see what Rose was doing. She was donning her outdoor gear.

"Where on earth are you going?" asked Emma, in surprise. "It's black as night out there."

"Don't worry, I'm not going far. I've found a torch so I'm just going up onto the hill above the farm, to see if I can get the mobile to at least send a message. Needless to say the main line isn't connected. Will you be alright for a short while?"

"Yes, I'll be fine. I'm just going to check out the bathroom, but I think it would be wise not to use the torch too much. I'd rather not advertise our whereabouts."

"No, I'll muffle it and be really careful. I don't expect I'll get a signal anyway. I just feel that I ought to have a go, as the others will be so worried." Rose, pink in the face, turned towards her and added, "The ghastly thing is Emma… that I broke the rule… I didn't tell anybody where I was going." She hesitated then with an anguished sigh finished, "Actually it was only because I was a bit pissed off with Oliver."

"Oh, I see." Emma replied. What else could she say? She'd exercised a little discretionary manipulation of plans herself.

"Anyway, I'll explain it all when I come back and then I'll get us something more to eat. I won't be long."

Emma lay back and luxuriated in her change of circumstances. In a strange way, she wanted to keep her escape to herself for a little longer, while she recovered her strength and made sure all was well with the baby. She didn't feel like facing the world again yet. She missed Marc of course, but she couldn't bear the thought of having to go over her whole ordeal to them all at the hotel, so soon after regaining her freedom. Rose had been extremely sensitive. She hadn't rushed her into recounting anything. It was almost as if she really understood her need to come to terms with everything that had happened first, while quietly snug, in this safe haven. Emma, rather selfishly, hoped that Rose wouldn't find a signal to alert the cavalry to their location; just for this one night. She needed longer to rest, to make sure she was alright and the time to tell Rose of her pregnancy.

The big dog had finished his meal. He lay beside the sofa, looking up at Emma approvingly, as if to concur with her thoughts. He looked very comfortable just where he was. Emma dropped her hand to stroke him and murmur endearments. He had probably saved her life. She wondered what his name was. He had a collar. She ran her fingers through his thick coat to see if she could find a disc. There was a name tag: she leant over to peer more closely at it.

"What's your name? Let's see now... 'Trost'... I wonder what that means? We'll ask Rose and see if her German is up to it. Sounds like 'trust'; that would be just perfect, wouldn't it?"

Rose returned, stamping her feet in the porch to remove all the excess snow and quickly shutting the door behind her against the wind. The fire discharged a puff of smoke from the draught.

"No go, I'm afraid. We are stuck here for the night. There's a huge amount of drifting, covering any prints and all signs of your amazing excursion up here, so you mustn't worry. Those evil people won't find us. We'll keep the curtains drawn and see by the firelight. Besides, it's freezing out there. Nobody in their right minds would venture out at this time of night. It must be the coldest night this year."

"Oh no, no it's not!" replied Emma with feeling, then continued, seeing the puzzled look on Rose's face.

"Tonight is not the coldest night of the year – no way. That was definitely last night."

"You're right, of course you're right," answered Rose understanding, "that must have been both the coldest and the worst night of your life. I just don't know how you survived it; you really have got true grit, haven't you?" Emma merely smiled.

"Well, quite honestly I can't think of a nicer place to recover. However I know that the others will now be worried about you as well as me."

"Yes," answered Rose. "And I can appreciate perhaps just a little of how you must feel after your ghastly experience. This place must really seem like a safe haven. There's no point in fussing about the others, as we can't do anything until the morning. So we might as well enjoy being here. Now first things first: food! I don't know about you, but I'm starving."

Rose found packets of soup and tins of Spaghetti Bolognaise which they could heat up on a griddle across the fire. They could finish with sliced yellow peaches in syrup.

"Good old Steffi, there's plenty to eat." Emma started to get up. "No," said Rose bossily. "You stay put just where you are. I don't want you passing out on me again."

"Alright, thanks Rose. As my mother would say, I'll accept with grace!"

Emma couldn't believe how hungry she was.

"Dear God! That went down fast, you must have been starving." Rose watched as the intrepid girl tipped out the last of the peach juice into her bowl. "Do you want some more? There's plenty of other stuff up on the shelf. Steffi won't mind one bit. She'd be delighted to come to our rescue." Emma laughed.

"No thanks. Sorry to be such a pig. That was just right. I feel so much better now. Mmm those peaches were delicious," she said licking her fingers.

Hunger assuaged and thirst quenched, they sat companionably in front of the fire. The heat bathed their faces with a healthy glow, inducing a sense of well-being, whilst the dog slept on.

"You know, it's a strange feeling," Emma said, eventually breaking the silence, "but after this particular experience, my life will never be the same again."

"Did you think that you were going to die?" asked Rose hoping that Emma would now confide in her and tell her the whole story.

"No, not unless I froze to death. I didn't think that they had it in them to kill me and anyway what would have been the point? I wouldn't have been much use to them dead. But I thought I'd be raped though, probably twice over and there's a reason why I couldn't possibly have let that happen: you see I'm three months pregnant." Rose stared dumbfounded, her eyes on stalks, then opened her mouth to speak but nothing came out.

"It's true," said Emma laughing. "I'm having a baby and poor Marc doesn't even know yet. I haven't had a chance to tell him. That's really the reason that I delayed in coming out and why it was all to be such a big surprise. Well, the big surprise went a bit wrong, didn't it?"

"Oh my God! I can't believe this," Rose replied recovering at last. "For heaven's sake Emma are you alright?"

"Yes, I think so. So far so good, no tummy pains or anything. The doctor said I was 'well on the way' and I feel much better now having been so perfectly looked after by you. I've slept loads and had a great meal, all thanks to you – and to Steffi of course," she added.

"You really are amazing, talk about the survival of the fittest." Rose came across to give her new friend a hug.

"Many, many congratulations Emma and I'm so lucky to be the first to know. Oh dear, I hope Marc won't mind; about me knowing, I mean. You needn't tell him you've told me."

"Of course he won't mind. He'll be so grateful to you for taking care of me. So you mustn't fret any more. I'll get my very own house doctor to check everything is alright, when we get back. Now... tell me how you came to find me, I'm dying to know." Rose, so admiring of the strength of this plucky woman, laughed.

"Okay, well... you'll never believe this but in actual fact the reason I'm here is because of our beautiful, four-legged, friend... let's see, what's his name?"

✳

Guy and Julian couldn't afford to wait any longer for Oliver. He'd obviously just missed a train and had to hang around longer than expected. He wasn't at the station when they got there and Zak's relation, with the snowmobile, was already in evidence, sheltering at the bus stop in the square nearby.

They parked the jeep in a little side road out of the way and, leaving the trusted cousin to wait for Olly with instructions for them to organize backup at the old deserted barn, they leapt on their transport and charged off out of the village, spewing up a fountain of white behind them. Zak's cousin went to warm up in the station waiting room while he waited for the next train, which was still ten minutes away.

There were no cars on the road now. Conditions were such that even the snow ploughs weren't in action until this particular storm had passed through. It was night time: no sensible people would be out and about now until morning. The trains, unaffected, continued for another few hours, to get everybody safely home and then emergencies would be catered for by snowmobile. They were fast and reliable.

Julian and Guy sped along the road, covering the two kilometres even quicker than in the jeep. At the turn off to the barn, at the beginning of the track, Guy stopped to check the red Mercedes. It was already half covered in snow.

"They'll have a job getting this to function much more tonight, let's see if there is anything of interest inside." Julian hadn't lost his touch: he had the door open in less than two minutes. Inside they found nothing but an empty cigarette packet, two tins of nearly finished Coca Cola and two half-eaten pizzas stuffed back in their boxes.

"Smells like a deli in here. Looks like they didn't have much of an appetite either, serves them right. God what a mess! Choice eating habits these people have, but at least they took the fourth pizza up with them, which is encouraging."

"How long a start do they have?" asked Guy. Julian checked his watch.

"Only thirty-five minutes and we should make up time on this far superior vehicle."

"Good, let's go then. It's a pity we have to use the lights, although the vision is so bad that if we can't see them, rest assured they can't see us and we also have the element of surprise with us. They won't be expecting us."

They muffled the lights, covering them with elasticized pieces of gauze and then set off following the already half obliterated trail made by the Iranians up ahead. It was an old farm track, offering a fairly obvious route up the mountain in spite of restricted vision and serious drifting. Guy hoped that before long they might recognize the lie of the land from summertime excursions. He felt sure now that they were closing the gap to Emma.

All his instincts told him that she was still alive but there was a fine balance between fact, intuitiveness and wishful thinking. Her captors were a pretty shoddy lot but, with their backs against the wall, could easily panic.

It was probably fortuitous that they'd left Oliver to help arrange things down below. They hadn't ever worked with him and he might just let them down unintentionally, through inexperience; besides which they'd have needed another machine.

Julian couldn't help smiling about how annoyed Olly would be at having been left behind. He really liked him and felt that he was somebody to be relied upon, although he had to admit to being a little nervous about leaving him alone pursuing the 'grey man'. Oliver could be a bit over enthusiastic. He just hoped that he didn't run into any kind of trouble while he was on his own.

* * *

CHAPTER 19

OLIVER was impatient. He'd obviously just missed the half-hourly train and had to wait for what seemed like an interminably long time until the next one which, in spite of the weather, came in punctually on the hour exactly as the time table had forecast.

The 'grey man', as he now named his quarry, had disappeared once more into the guest house, just before Oliver had left his surveillance post at the café opposite. It had been a good spot and he'd managed to grab a hot mug of coffee and a piece of cake, at the same time as he'd picked up the train timetable. The woman serving seemed to know everything about the area and was pleased to tell him, showing off her reasonable command of English. When the Iranian had come in for the coffee, she'd clicked her tongue in disapproval, as he'd left without thanking her. Before Oliver had set off after him, when he'd gone to pay, she'd told him that she hadn't liked the look of the man and that there were plenty of other languages in which to say thank you. Olly had politely agreed and couldn't help wondering what her reaction would have been had she known just how accurate her insight had been. How very different was the softly spoken, distinguished-looking scientist up the mountain, in comparison with his villainous pursuers.

As Oliver waited for the passengers to get off, he watched as a large party of noisy, macho skiers spilled out of the first two carriages. Mostly young men, they were dressed in full bad-weather gear and still had snow on their boots with even a sprinkling on some of their hats. This hardened group were obviously awesome sportsmen, guessed Oliver. Most likely they were local, or at least knew the mountain very well indeed, because they must have skied down in the dark. Two of the men, who appeared to be in charge of the group, had powerful lights strapped around their foreheads. Quite an exciting adventure they must have had in near blizzard conditions.

He hopped on the train just as the last man got out and sat down watching all the pink-faced young people setting off to wherever they were going to spend their evening. Just as the station master was about to wave them away, a man appeared at the run and jumped up into the next carriage. It was the grey man! 'God thought Oliver, who exactly is following who?'

He took out his mobile and quickly sent a message to Guy. An answer came almost straight back. 'Stay with him if you can and report progress.' They drew into the next station. Olly got up and went to the door to watch. The grey man got out and Oliver followed, getting out discreetly with two small children and their mother whom he helped with the push chair.

The Iranian was buttoning up his coat against the elements and heading off at a brisk walk out of the village. 'Where the hell is he going' wondered Oliver, tapping in another report to Guy. 'I can't very well go on foot, in pursuit along the road: much too obvious.' The man disappeared around a left hand bend. Oliver stood deliberating then endeavoured to send a follow-up message to Guy. It was hard to see in the dark; it was snowing heavily again making everything wet. It took three attempts and precious minutes to get the text off; he was in a hurry and he always hit the wrong key if he tried to rush it. Oliver swore in exasperation. It was so cold that his fingers were numb, making things even more difficult. He'd just finished texting and had the 'message sent' verified, when he noticed a four-by-four, parked facing him in the entrance to a little side road. The driver flashed the lights twice and a man stepped out of the car and beckoned: a man in a mackintosh, who he immediately recognized, silhouetted against the street light. Julian: great. He'd had enough of surveillance on his own and was looking forward to seeing the others again. A renewed surge of adrenalin kicked in as Oliver began quickly to walk towards the car, anticipating and wondering about their next move. This really was turning out to be one hell of a day.

✳

As the English party filed in through the hotel entrance Hélène walked across from the reception desk to meet them.

"Rose did go up the other side of the mountain," Hélène announced breathlessly, confirming their suspicions. "Apparently she went up at about two-thirty this afternoon, bought a map and seemed particularly interested in the new lift."

"God! What does Rose think she's doing? What an idiot going up there in this appalling weather," Alicia burst out, seriously rattled.

"Let alone going out without telling any of us," Adriana added, for good measure. "She's broken the most fundamental of ski rules."

"There's no point in getting annoyed," Marc said, sensibly. "The thing is that we now have another missing person, so let's decide what we should do about it?" He looked to Hélène for inspiration.

"Well… first, I've talked to Steffi. The road up the mountain is, as I thought, completely closed off. The drifting is too heavy even for the snowploughs to bother, with nobody living up there. Besides which there are also some trees that have been brought down in the blizzard. It's hopeless trying to get up to the farm that way. Secondly, the weather is so bad that they are not prepared to reopen the lift again until morning, as it would only endanger others and I'm afraid the helicopter can't fly either. The local man, who checks that the pistes are empty last thing, says he is prepared to take a snow-mobile up the mountain, to the top, to see if he can see any sign of her. Otherwise, with the weather so hazardous, there is nothing more to be done until the morning. I'm really sorry," she finished lamely. She had been extremely efficient but was obviously deeply upset. Nobody spoke for a minute. Then Hélène offered one last small piece of encouragement.

"The piste man did also say that Rose appeared to be a very competent skier. Someone saw her setting off from the top."

Hélène was an expert skier herself and of course also knew the area better than anybody. She had grown up here. The young woman looked at all the gloomy faces and continued, trying to be encouraging,

"If she has gone off piste she might have happened on one of the deserted farm buildings up there: if she was lucky. Perhaps that side of the valley is a little more sheltered. In spite of the storm the wind has dropped now and, for the moment at least, it's not quite so cold. Last night recorded the coldest night to date. Rose was apparently dressed very warmly and also had a back-pack. Even in a makeshift shelter, lower down, she should survive the night alright, if she's sensible, which I'm sure she is." Hélène's voice trailed off.

"I really am sorry," she said again, knowing that none of this information was particularly welcome, "but that's all they could say. It's most unusual as normally when someone is lost the helicopter automatically goes out, but I suppose that at present the visibility is just so atrocious they don't want to risk anybody else. Oh dear, poor Rose. I do hope she's alright." Hélène sank down into a chair exhausted with the worry of it all and with having had to be the bearer of such bad news.

Marc went and stood beside her, placing a reassuring hand on her shoulder as he did so. Two other guests wandered past, obviously wondering what was going on, perhaps sensing the charged atmosphere. Hélène hastily jumped up, pulling herself together enough to politely say "Hello and good evening." Alicia and Adriana, talking quietly, were moving away from the reception area for privacy. They didn't want all Hélène's other guests to be unnecessarily upset.

"Backpack… she had a backpack. What about the mobile, did she take it?" Alicia asked looking intently at Adriana.

"It wasn't in her room, but I doubt there would be a signal up there anyway."

"Never mind, let's at least try text messaging. It worked eventually for us up this side of the mountain the other day." The two girls thanked Hélène, who looked somewhat relieved when they went to sit at a table further away. Marc remained standing rather forlornly, with his hands thrust deep in his pockets; he let out a long sigh.

"What a nightmare it all is," he said, his normally smiling face creased with strain.

"It's worst of all for you, Marc," replied Hélène tiredly, her usual exuberance also faltering momentarily.

"I just don't know how you can remain so calm, you poor man. It really must be so awful for you, wondering all the time what's happening to Emma."

"Ah well... I think it's just the positive mentality of the doctor in me which helps most of the time," he said, tapping his head, as he prepared to join the girls. "The training keeps things more or less in control, but it is a pretty grim situation."

"You won't let anybody else out of your sight now, will you?" implored Hélène inclining her head to where the two girls were sitting.

"No, of course not," Marc reassured shaking his head, "not a chance... but you'll let me know if you hear anything?"

"Yes, certainly, I will let you know straight away if I hear anything at all. I promise."

"Thank you Hélène, thank you very much indeed. No matter what the outcome, you have been wonderful." He gave her a hug.

"You're more than welcome," Hélène replied. "I just wish I had some good news to give you. I am so very fond of both Rose and Emma. But you mustn't become despondent. Rose is strong and intrepid and Emma, as we all know from past experience, is brave and shrewd. They both have everything to live for and Emma was so excited about surprising you." Nearly in tears after her emotional speech, Hélène, with a catch in her throat, managed a smile then moved off to look after a guest needing her at the reception desk.

✳ ✳ ✳

CHAPTER 20

UP on the mountain the storm continued to rage. The wind howled furiously and pieces of debris were blowing around outside, sometimes eerily skidding across the roof or knocking at the windows.

"Heavens, I'm glad we're not out in that," said Emma with feeling.

"It's as if there are aliens out there trying to force open the door, sort of tormenting us." Rose sounded wistful. She looked up at Emma frowning, "I'm going to be in such trouble when we get back. Olly will be livid with me as will the others. Quite rightly, they will think I'm thoroughly irresponsible for going off without telling them." She turned to Emma, "Perhaps I'll hide out here a bit longer."

"Don't be silly. They'll all be so pleased to see us both safe. And anyway, I'll stick up for you. I think that I shall be able to cope with anything and anybody now, after this lot."

"It's not the first time that you have been in a violent situation, is it?"

Emma appeared surprised.

"No, it's not. But how did you know that?"

"Oh! Just something you said earlier and also one night at dinner Marc was singing your praises and saying what an exceptionally brave person you are, particularly after some nasty incident when apparently you saved the day, so to speak. Do you want to talk about it? I'd love to hear the full story."

"Ah! Yes! 'The Ionian Incident' as we call it. Alright, seeing as we have all night, why not! It was in Greece when I first met Marc, when we fell in love actually, but it was someone else's life at stake on that occasion, not mine and…" she said patting her stomach, "I didn't have this to worry about either."

Rose settled back against the cushions, putting all her thoughts about next day's difficulties to the back of her mind, while contentedly she listened to Emma's soft voice recalling her story, set under the olives in Greece.

Emma was quite happy to talk the night away. She was warm and safe from harm now. It was just too bad that Marc and the others had another worrying night ahead. But they hadn't been through the ordeal she had and she needed this time, the peace and the companionship of Rose who, against all odds, had found and looked after her. In spite of everything this was a strange unplanned yet special time for the two new friends, and both women, for their different reasons, were in fact thankful that there was no telephone in working order.

❋

Oliver screwed up his eyes as a blast of wind blew a flurry of snow in his face. He didn't see the man walking purposely fast towards him from the direction of the station and trying to catch him up. He hurried on across the square, intent on getting out of the bad weather and joining the others.

The passenger door of the jeep was thrown open for him and with relief he leapt in. Oliver heard the door locks click shut securely around him. Just for a split second he wondered about that, then he turned to Julian. But… it wasn't Julian or Guy. It was the 'grey man' and he had a gun in his hand, pointing directly at Oliver's head.

'Fucking bloody hell, I've blown it,' thought the young Englishman in a surprisingly fearless fury.

❊

Guy slowed down as they approached some farm buildings which he didn't, so far, recognize. It was a small-holding with only one separate outhouse. The cow barn, as in many cases in this country, was built onto the end of the house. The tracks they were following went through the courtyard and on up the mountain.

"We'll stop here for a minute; see if my mobile works. I want to call both Zak and Olly." They edged in under the lintel of the house for shelter. Julian looked out at the bleak, ever darkening landscape, while Guy took out his phone. The sky and ground were as one; a blur of the same cold, dank grey. The wind had dropped but the snow continued to fall, silently and relentlessly. Guy broke the quietness by stabbing in the numbers on his mobile. Julian stretched his long limbs then shifted his weight to lean against the building, the better to hear. Guy was listening intently. Zak obviously had some news to impart and it didn't sound good. The recipient swore several times and Julian caught the gist of the conversation. The tables had been turned. The grey man had Olly and the jeep. Guy closed his phone and stashed it away in his pocket. He remained still for a minute, contemplating the changed situation, before he spoke.

"You heard that?" Julian nodded.

"Most of it. Poor old Olly, but he's not dead yet, so don't give up on the poor sod."

"No, of course not: but what an idiot: inexperience. My fault though. Maybe I was a fool for bringing him in. The grey man, in hijacking the jeep, is cleverer than I had thought. He's definitely a cut above the other two goons. Anyway, Zak is on his way down to help; he has enough people to leave up there with our scientist friend. Everybody has the jeep's description. It will be easy to track in this weather. There won't be many vehicles out and about. There's nothing we can do for Olly at the moment: we must continue on up as planned and hope that he can find a way to extract himself, otherwise they'll use him as a pawn as well... damn and blast. How in hell did he let that happen?"

Guy removed his hat and shook the snow off it. His dark hair was damp and curly with the heat from his head, encased in the wool. His blue eyes were focused and his mouth was set determinedly. He was good at this job; better than anybody else he knew, reflected Julian, watching his friend rearranging the plans in his mind. Guy was upset about Oliver and he felt responsible for his abduction, but it really wasn't his fault. These things happen. Oliver was aware of the danger involved in this operation. He wanted 'in'. The fact that he'd been taken was purely and simply bad luck. Julian much preferred being second in command. He was happy for Guy to take the difficult decisions particularly, as in this case, when their friends were in the firing line.

"Olly will be alright, you'll see. I'm not usually wrong in my character assessment of people in this job," was all Julian said as he moved from his position propped against the wooden door and prepared to remount the snowmobile. Guy said nothing and merely hoped that Julian's faith would prove justified.

❋

"We can't just sit here doing nothing all evening." Alicia was feeling inadequate, two people were missing: there must be something they could do. Marc was scribbling on a scrap of paper and Adriana stared into space, miles away, with an untouched cup of coffee on the table in front of her. Silence prevailed, except for the monotonous sound of the pencil scratching on the piece of card. Then Adriana returned to the present.

"The men will be furious if we don't do as we are told and stay here, but I've been thinking..." Oh no! Marc, who was sitting opposite, realized that she had a plan in the making. Adriana's eyes were sparkling once more, full of enthusiasm, as an idea took hold. She really is a very sexy girl, he thought remembering their shared intimacy only a short time ago. She positively oozed sex appeal. He also felt that if he were Julian he'd marry her fast before someone else came along and snapped her up. No man could pass by without a second look. Even feeling how he was at the moment he couldn't help but find her attractive. Adriana sat up straight and launched forth.

"I agree with Ally. We can't just stay here in the hotel and twiddle our thumbs. How about we go down to the town for dinner tonight? We can go by train; it's only three stops from here."

"That's a brilliant plan and we could ask if anyone has seen Rose at the same time. What do you think Marc?" Marc shifted uneasily in his chair.

"Well, I suppose we could, as long as we take the mobiles – and make sure they are charged," he added, looking pointedly, across at Alicia. Adriana was getting more excited by the minute.

"There is another possibility to consider in these atrocious weather conditions. Maybe Rose did come down the mountain into the village of Blumenstein, but instead of coming back here by train she went the other way to the main town and the shops."

"You're right, it is quite likely. She might have gone to the thermal baths even. She was so pissed off with us and with Olly. There's no harm in our going there to ask, is there?" Adriana got up, "Come on Marc, come with us. Of all people it will do you good to get out."

"Alright, I suppose so. But we'll tell Hélène where we will be for dinner, so she can get hold of us. I'll ask her to book a table at the Italian restaurant. You probably know it?" They both nodded.

"Good. Then let's meet back here at seven o'clock. There's usually a train at a quarter past the hour going that way. I'll pick up a time-table from reception, for coming back."

The girls went up the stairs together. Alicia stopped on the landing. She turned to Adriana.

"You don't think that there could possibly be any connection between Rose's disappearance and Emma's abduction, do you?" There was silence as Adriana contemplated this suggestion.

"Well," she answered, "I have to admit that I am beginning to wonder just a little bit, but I didn't like to say anything in front of Marc."

"Personally, I think it's unlikely," answered Alicia. "But perhaps we shouldn't abandon the idea altogether."

They stood for a moment dwelling on this latest theory. Adriana's face lit up, she wanted some action.

"I agree, but guess what? I've still got Rose's key," she said conspiratorially, "I think she has a picture of herself with Olly on the dressing table. I noticed it earlier. Let's go and see; it could prove helpful."

Marc wasn't quite so keen on the plan but at least it would keep him from indulging in negative thoughts. Where? Oh where was his beloved wife? Pray to every God on the planet that his trust in Guy and Julian was well placed and that they would find her safe and well. Much had happened during this turbulent day; it seemed such a long time since his dreadful, early morning wake-up call.

* * *

CHAPTER 21

OLIVER was made to drive. The grey man sat without speaking, but with his gun aimed somewhere in the region of Olly's heart. As they began back down the road in the direction of Speigelsee, Oliver considered his options. Should he sit tight for the moment, or should he fake loss of control of the jeep on the slippery road? If he did, they could land up in the ditch together and the gun might go off by mistake: bad idea he concluded. His mobile had rung twice; the man had snatched it out of his pocket and turned it off, at the same time as he had removed Olly's own gun and the spare magazine of ammunition.

Oliver thought that, all in all, the best thing for the moment was to do as he was told, while using the time to assess the character of the man at the helm. In the Territorial Army he'd sat in on a lecture once, which had been about teaching the soldiers how to deal with hostage situations. He'd found it fascinating. 'Humour the man or men,' they'd been taught. 'No matter what, we are all human; and providing we have the God-given faculties, we all have emotions, so keep your head down and humour those feelings. Build up a relationship if you can and most importantly bide your time.' Yes, thought Olly, it's all very well, but building up a relationship when you don't speak the same language isn't so easy. He wasn't frightened; not really. He was too busy being annoyed with himself for being caught and wondering how the hell he could outwit this very grey, silent Iranian adversary.

The man smelt of sweat and he'd been smoking. The acrid stench still clung to his clothes. Guy loathed the smell of smoke in the car; Julian was always getting into trouble. The thought of this person having a fag, in Guy's jeep, struck Oliver as quite funny and without thinking he let out a chuckle as he drove. The grey man looked amazed that the Englishman should find anything amusing, considering his unfavourable situation.

So far, the man didn't appear to have the wish to indulge in unnecessary violence but he was visibly nervous behind the calm exterior and could snap at any time, thought Olly. He must use these notions to his own advantage.

They arrived back in the town, where he had to park the four-by-four behind an old warehouse near the station. The man communicated by gesticulating frantically and digging Olly unnecessarily in the ribs. He didn't need words, so he didn't bother to use them. It was good to be out in the air again, despite the driving snow, away from the enclosed confines of the jeep. Olly latched onto a mild returning sense of security as he walked along in someone else's half-covered footsteps. There were people in the vicinity who might just possibly come to his aid, if he could just orchestrate a suitable manoeuvre.

Oliver guessed that they were headed back to the guest house. Except for the one pair of half-obliterated footprints, there was no sign of life in this part of the town, away from the bright lights in the main street and the shops. It was about as down-trodden an area in Switzerland as you could find; deserted railway sidings and long, low buildings, probably used for train servicing. There was no buzzing station hotel with its little bistro which could usually be found in most Swiss towns.

They walked quickly along dark, deserted, narrow side streets until they turned into a road which he recognized. The café was on the far side. Oliver looked across hopefully wondering and rather hoping that the woman in charge might notice them pass by. If she saw them together she'd find it odd to see him in the company of that 'rude foreigner'. Unfortunately, the windows were all fogged up.

"It's cold," he said, shivering to make his meaning clear. The grey man shrugged, seeming to understand and hurried him on. He had the gun uncomfortably stuck into Oliver's side, as they walked on together towards their destination. Oliver imagined, but couldn't be sure, that the gun was loaded: best to assume it was.

"Whoops," Olly pretended to slip to delay things a bit, while they still were level with the café. He wasn't looking forward to becoming a prisoner, shut up in a room, away from people and he was hoping that someone might come out into the street. If they did, perhaps he could pretend they were a friend and call a greeting as a distraction. But nobody left the warmth of the little restaurant, which was most likely a good thing, as an incident might also have put others in danger. In the TA they were taught not to instigate any action that might further endanger life.

Soon they were entering a large, square, modern-looking building. It was grey. Everything seemed grey presently, thought Oliver, except for a neon sign hung above the entrance depicting a festive cow with a head-dress of flowers. Incongruously, Olly remembered seeing the animals dressed in such a colourful way, when they came down in procession off their summer pastures in September. When the front door shut behind them, he felt rattled for the first time.

There was no light and no sound from inside the guest house. Their intrusion seemed loud in the silent building. It was either very empty or everyone was out in the town. The automatic switch clicked on loudly, bathing the passage in fluorescent illumination. There were several rooms on the ground floor, all with hand-painted, tastefully decorated plates on the door with the name of a mountain flower. Oliver dragged his feet, wishing that someone would come out of their room, initiating perhaps possible means of escape. He was dug in the ribs yet again by the man with the gun; he winced, his side already sore. This needless action was becoming irritating, to say the least. After all he was hardly likely to argue with the gun. *"Boro ballah,"* was all the grey man muttered indicating that Olly should ascend the stairs. They went up two floors and stopped by the door, at the end of the corridor, named Hyazinthe. Odd how some of the words in German were almost the same as English ones, Oliver mused. The door was unlocked and Olly was unceremoniously shoved inside. With the light on he then turned slowly around to scrutinize his adversary and his surroundings properly.

The Iranian couldn't hold Oliver's gaze. He removed Julian's mackintosh, revealing a dark jersey and a pair of jeans beneath. His hair was black and dishevelled. He had dark, hawk-like eyes, a crooked nose and thin, mean-looking lips above a small, immature goatee beard. Oliver imagined he was normally clean shaven and most likely the stubble was grown for practical reasons whilst on this job, but more importantly to hide behind. He was always suspicious of men with facial hair. Olly's captor now stood with the gun held threateningly, deliberately sliding the safety catch to 'off', then obviously feeling more secure favoured Oliver with the same detailed scrutiny. Olly noticed the nervous tick at the outside corner of the man's left eye and the hand that held the weapon was just not quite steady. The room smelt, like his captor, of stale sweat: Oliver imagined the window never being opened. His brain received a message: 'remember, take your time laddie, put the man at ease'; so Olly smiled at the grey man. He was rewarded with a startled grunt then pushed into a chair and told to stay, or so Olly understood: *"Vaystah"* the man snarled.

It was hot in the room. Olly asked politely if he might take off his coat. The man nodded consent, then removed the belt from the mac and proceeded to inexpertly bind the Englishman's wrists, avoiding Oliver's eyes on such close contact as he did so. Oliver sat down at the oblong table and was then left to ponder his situation while his gaoler got out his mobile. The man walked around the table and glanced across at Oliver. Then, turning his back, maybe to seek a little privacy, made his call. As if Olly could understand a word of the Farsi language anyway: what a hope!

"Chi shodeh, chi shodeh." Then there was silence while the man listened; something was obviously wrong. Oliver at least understood this much, hoping that maybe Guy and Julian were on the case and had managed somehow to upset the Iranians' plans. Perhaps they'd found Emma. Oliver's ears were straining to comprehend the gist of the conversation as his eyes bore into the back of the grey man. There was an exasperated intake of breath, followed by much obvious swearing. A heated conversation ensued with most likely, Olly thought, one of the other two ruffians who had taken Emma.

Olly could once again imagine his commanding officer in the TA hissing in his ear, 'bide your time boyo, bide your time'. The man might pause for prayer before long, he hoped. His aggressor was certainly fanatical and this might offer Olly an opportunity to escape. Surely his captor wouldn't forego his religious beliefs because of the present situation? If Oliver remembered correctly, the Iranian should pray five times a day. He glanced out of the window: it was well past sunset but he had no idea of the time. There just might be one more prayer session to go, if he was lucky. The man's attention would be distracted, then Olly would be in with a chance. The belt around his wrists had already loosened. He hadn't been thoroughly searched either when he was captured or since they'd entered the room. He still had his knife, tucked neatly in between his sock and his boot. His adversary wasn't a professional or he would have found it.

Oliver experienced a wave of controlled optimism. Every sense was alert; he felt strong and able. He knew with absolute certainty that he was capable of outwitting this man. The tide was turning: it was merely a question of finding the right moment and using that essential element, surprise, to achieve his freedom.

✳

"What weather! I've never seen so much snow," cried Alicia jumping down from the train in front of the others. Her boots sank into a drift about a foot deep.

"Yes, it seems worse than ever. It's late so let's go straight to the restaurant," Marc suggested.

"Good idea," agreed Adriana. "There's no sense in trekking around in this. Let's have dinner, then when we are feeling fortified we can start asking around. For instance, there's a little café over there I don't remember noticing before." She pointed to the brave little light, shining brightly above the door, advertising the bistro. "We can go in there just before we leave and show them the picture: just in case anyone remembers seeing Rose."

206

CHAPTER 22

GUY and Julian saw the pin pricks of light ahead in the same instant. The torches were moving back and forth, as if searching for something, in an agitated fashion. Guy stopped the snowmobile and killed their own dim headlights.

"That's the farm a couple of miles below Steffi's isn't it?"

"I'm not sure, until we get a bit closer," Julian answered. "I can't quite recognize where we are for the moment, coming in from this direction and with all of the usual landmarks covered over."

"No, but as I remember there's nothing else at this level. When we walked down this side, from the top in the summer a few years ago, there was a track which had a steep incline and twisted and turned but eventually linked both farms."

The two men stood for a few minutes considering their next move.

"I think we'd better walk from here." They dismounted and hid their transport behind some snow-laden bushes.

"God, I hope we'll find it again, with all this snow." Julian glanced across at his friend, unable to conceal a grin. "You really do look like the original abominable snow man, you know!"

"You look pretty good yourself," Guy replied, knocking a lump off Julian's black, wool hat. "We'll go on up the track for a bit. It will be easier to see and then we can dive off into the wood, when we get near." He looked upwards. "I think it's easing off just a little. A bit of help from the moon wouldn't go amiss. I don't want to have to use any other kind of light to announce our arrival."

The two men checked for markers to re-locate the hidden machine and tramped on through the thick drifts. In spite of the weather, there was a translucent, eerie glow created by the thick blanket of whiteness on which the foreigners' tracks were still just visible. Ten minutes later they could see the outline of a large barn roof in the distance with its conspicuous weather vane. The torch lights appeared to have stopped searching and were now almost stationary. Guy looked behind him. It was snowing heavily again. This on-going storm had its advantages and disadvantages. In this case it was the former. They had been following in the Iranians' faint snowmobile indentations and already even their own most recent footprints were barely distinguishable.

"OK, I think it's time to divert now," said Guy stepping sideways into the wood and almost immediately merging into the gloom.

"They could be on the move again. What do you want to do then?" Julian was itching now for some action.

"Let them go by. Zak's team will have organized a reception party at the bottom by now." He checked his watch. "I think Emma is up here and she's first priority."

They trudged slowly on, carefully avoiding branches and any other hazards which might advertise their presence. They came to the farm clearing and ducked down behind some bushes at the edge of the forest. The big barn loomed in front of them, across the courtyard. A skimobile was parked outside and the two men were rummaging around inside. The torchlight was flashing around frantically and the men were arguing volubly.

"Emma can't be in there," whispered Julian, "The door is broken down. Look!"

"Yes, so I see, but what the hell are they doing then?"

"Probably just covering their tracks and clearing up... she could be trussed up in a corner I suppose, poor thing." Julian muttered. He wasn't going to add 'or dead'.

"She'd freeze to death, unable to move around in these conditions," Guy growled. "I just hope to God they haven't done anything they will seriously regret." At this point, and for the first time, he was beginning to think that they might, after all, find a body.

The snow had stopped momentarily, but a bitter wind had got up instead, blowing it around in flurries. Julian looked up through a gap in the trees. Clouds scudded across the sky and for a moment there was the vague glimmer of a partially obscured coy moon.

"Watch it! They're coming out." Guy crouched down lower.

Two figures emerged into the dim light, silhouetted against a huge drift at the side of the barn entrance. Guy and Julian could hear the murmur of voices, raised slightly in disagreement. There was much gesticulating and then one of the men got out his phone, holding it up for better reception. There was silence while he waited for the call to be answered and then another heated discussion ensued. The second man paced around, kicking at the snow in agitation, then undid his fly to urinate up against the broken barn door.

The telephone conversation finished, the man with the mobile swore loudly, shouted at his fellow countryman and jumped onto their transport in readiness for their descent.

The noise of the furiously revving machine tore into the stillness of the night. The Iranians were in such a hurry to leave that they very nearly came to grief getting back over the incline and onto the track. With far too much acceleration, the vehicle bucked its way over the mounds of snow, almost depositing both its graceless occupants in a heap.

"Bloody idiots," remarked Julian chuckling.

Guy was quiet, as the snowmobile floundered its way past. He concentrated his mind on the meaning of the small scene they'd just witnessed. They waited until the receding light had disappeared around a bend before moving.

"Things aren't going quite according to plan, that's quite obvious," Guy remarked, fishing in his pocket for his own mobile. "The phone works here. I'll just warn Zak's people that they are on their way down, then we'd better have a look inside the barn."

The two men were silent as they made their way across the clearing then stood outside listening for a moment before entering.

"Right let's get it over with. If Emma's still in here I reckon the ultimate filthy deed is already done; it's too quiet." Julian sighed, stepping inside, fearing the worst.

They stood in the middle of the great building, looking around, taking in every little detail. No body: a biscuit tin lid, an apple core and an empty water bottle stood partly concealed beside an obvious impression where someone had lain in the straw. A scrap of torn woman's clothing was tied around the bottle top. There were deep ruts and mud where a big machine had rested against one side of the barn not long before. The wheel indentations ran towards the big double doors which had been forcefully broken down. The newly splintered wood lay in heaps, covered in snow, all around the entrance. The two Englishmen stood gaping at each other for some moments, stunned into silence as they absorbed the astonishing evidence laid bare before them.

"My God!" exclaimed Guy finally. "Emma was here and what's more she's escaped."

"And by the look of it, on a ruddy great piece of farm machinery as well."

Guy walked across to remove the small piece of cloth from around the neck of the water bottle. 'Made in Scotland', the tab stated firmly and reassuringly. He handed it to Julian.

"But where the hell has she got to now?" Guy spread his hands indicating bewilderment.

"And in these fucking awful conditions as well… God Almighty, what a girl!" Julian was grinning from ear to ear with relief.

❉

Nobody felt particularly hungry, but Marc insisted they all ate warm comforting pasta and drank good Italian chianti, which did indeed cheer them all up a bit and restore their flagging energy.

The girls were quiet as they ate, busy with their own thoughts and Marc was at least pleased to be in the restaurant and away from the hotel for a while. It was difficult there; with everybody knowing about his wife's abduction. The people he passed on his way to and from his room and in the other areas of the hotel always tried to politely avert their eyes, but curiosity usually got the better of them. They had to see how he was faring, probably to report back to others in their party. Human nature, he supposed, but irritating in the extreme.

As a doctor based in the UK Marc was used to ministering to the general public and, on occasion, even dealing with the press. But now this all seemed another world away. His private life was in the limelight and at present he didn't appreciate his likeness to a goldfish, albeit one enclosed in a very comfortable and charming bowl. He would just give anything for life to return to normal and to have Emma sitting safely beside him, where she should be.

"A penny for them?" Adriana had caught the look of raw anguish in his eyes. She laid a hand gently on his arm and added quietly, "Seriously Marc we can only imagine what you are be going through. It must be absolute hell, but all I can say is that both Ally and I have total confidence in the capabilities of our men. If anybody can bring this whole ghastly saga to a satisfactory conclusion, they can. Let's face it, we all know how experienced they are." She glanced across at her friend for confirmation. "Isn't that right Ally?"

"Absolutely it is," Alicia answered without hesitation. "Actually…" she continued, "for the moment Rose worries me almost as much. If she's cut off up there, somewhere with no shelter…" her voice trailed off.

"Alright," interrupted Marc, "enough of this. If everybody has finished eating, let's pay the bill and get out there."

They tried all the usual haunts: restaurants, bars, even the salt baths, which were closed and in the process of being cleaned; but nobody had seen or heard of Rose. Finally, despondent, the three friends set off back to the station. The weather had improved slightly and there were more people around now. A group of French teenagers passed them by in high spirits, fresh out of some drinking place, and began to run around throwing snowballs at each other. One missile, probably on purpose, narrowly missed Adriana. She ducked and laughed out loud; she always drew attention with her tumbling, tawny-coloured hair and voluptuous figure. On another occasion they might all have joined in. The youngsters moved on in the direction of the café, its bright light advertising a warm welcome.

"The café," Alicia exclaimed. "We haven't checked the café."

"Okay, but we better make it quick or we'll miss the last train," Marc replied as he and Adriana hurried after her.

It was hot and steamy inside the room, with the smell of pastry cooking and a slight lingering aroma of stewed coffee. Perhaps after a quiet night the chef was already baking for the next morning's customers. The teenagers were all settling themselves in a corner taking off their wet clothes and shaking the snow all over the floor. Alicia went straight over to the lady in charge behind the till. She appeared unfazed by the group, had a block of paper and a pen in her hand and was cheerfully preparing to collect the young people's orders. Her boss would be pleased with these late customers boosting a quiet day's business.

Alicia grabbed the picture from her pocket and interrupting as politely as possible asked:

"*Entschuldigung*, I'm so sorry but we need to ask you something before catching the next train. Do you speak English?" The café waitress nodded proudly in assent. Alicia glanced quickly at her watch and then shoved the picture of Rose and Olly under the woman's nose.

"Have you by any chance seen this girl around here today? It's really important to us, if you have."

The woman looked first at Alicia and then at her two friends. Olga liked the English and this girl was upset, undoubtedly very distressed about something. She glanced down at the picture and studied the face of the pretty, dark girl in the frame. She shook her head.

"*Nein nein, es tut mir leid… wie schade.*" Olga was sorry not to be able to help these nice people. She looked again into the man's face and saw suffering, well embedded, behind his unusual, flecked, brown eyes. She wished she could help and there was something familiar about the picture… what was it?

"*Eine minute bitte,*" she said taking back the photograph to study it more closely. Marc stopped thinking about missing the train; he could sense a shift in the atmosphere – they all could. The lady knew something. Both the girls leant closer, almost holding their breath, while they waited.

Olga looked up at the troubled trio, standing alert over the far side of the counter, hardly able to contain their impatience. She had something to tell them. She hoped it would help remove some of the anxiety from the faces of the three strangers. She glanced down once more to make certain, then took a deep breath. Now it was time to show off her English and this she felt to be important.

"The girl, *nein*" she said tapping the frame, "*nur* the man, he came here today to eat my strudel, very polite. He went with another, a foreigner, not a good man I think, *nein*, a bad man," she said shaking her head, remembering and glancing behind her at the ornate cuckoo clock on the wall above her head. "Maybe two hours ago; they went by here to the *gästezimmer,* on the

216

other side of the road." She pointed, indicating the opposite side of the street, returning to judge the reaction of her rapt audience which stood waiting, their young faces eager with expectation.

Olga was rewarded. She'd heard the intake of breath. The three English people before her, for the moment at least, seemed to be struck dumb. Perhaps now they'd stay and have some hot restoring tea and a piece of her very Scottish shortbread. Then she could tell them her opinion of the very rude, rough-looking, foreigner who had never said thank you and who appeared to have made off with their friend.

❋   ❋   ❋

CHAPTER 23

"I THINK we need to go back down," said Guy, looking around the barn while considering their next move.

"But what about Emma? Where on earth do you think she's got to?" asked Julian. Guy let out a low amused chuckle.

"Christ alone knows! But if Emma has managed to escape from these people, by forcing her way out of this barn on a bloody great piece of farm machinery, then she is more than capable of surviving the rest of the night. She even had the foresight to tear off a scrap of her clothing before she left and to leave it where we would be bound to find it. How brilliant a move was that? She's alright for the moment, she's won her freedom and I reckon that by now she has a pretty good idea of where she is. She's been over here in the summer. The best thing that we can do now is get down to the bottom fast and make sure that her abductors are off her case. Then we can re-plan and concentrate the search."

"You're right. But what about Olly and the Iranian boss?"

"Yes, we need to think about that too. Zak may have an update. First things first, let's get these two out of the way, then we can find Olly and his grey man. Come on, it's after midnight, let's go. We've already wasted enough time here: another couple of hours and it will be getting light."

They set off down the track in pursuit of Emma's captors, their journey made easier by the newly beaten tracks in the snow. An incandescent glimmer of moon now showed its reluctant face, lighting their way down and promising better weather. The storm was finally moving off.

❄

Zak, with three friends from the Cantonal police force, had no trouble at all in scooping up the two conspicuous foreign men on their stolen snowmobile. Emma's kidnappers were in an agitated state and quite unaware of the reception party waiting hidden behind some bushes, close by their snow-covered Mercedes. They were already in trouble for losing the English girl and were hoping, unbeknown to their boss, to get out of the area and away before dawn. As they skidded to a halt they were leapt upon, thrown to the ground and disarmed, all in a matter of seconds.

By the time Guy and Julian appeared the two terrified individuals were standing despondently, nicely trussed and propped up against the car, while their captors were discussing the jeep, which had been spotted down in the main town of Spiegelsee, near the station.

"Well done," said Guy. "Now who is it here that speaks Farsi?" One of the policemen raised his hand and came forward. "Good, now to save time…" he beckoned to Zak, "let's get them inside this old barn and find out everything we need to know."

❄

Annoyingly, there had been no final prayer session but Oliver had made a plan. He was getting stiff and wondered if he'd be allowed to stand in order to stretch his limbs. He'd noticed a heavy fire extinguisher on the floor within his reach and he needed to get a better view from the window which looked out onto the street. The grey man was exceedingly fussed. He was pacing the floor and constantly checking his mobile, presumably for messages. Surely, by now, someone had a trace on these mobiles? Their plans were obviously going belly up. Oliver wondered where his own mobile had got to. Perhaps it was still in the jeep or in the man's coat pocket. He longed to know what had happened and felt that now was probably the right time to act, while the man was so very distracted. The gun was on the other end of the table and he'd managed to loosen his constraints even more. He could now move both hands individually.

Oliver coughed to get the man's attention and indicated that he wished to stand and stretch his legs. His captor appeared irritated at the intrusion to his thoughts, but put the mobile down beside the gun on the table, got out a cigarette and nodded to Oliver to go ahead. Olly stood up gingerly, pretending extreme stiffness. After all, he must have been sitting for a couple of hours. He smiled his thanks and the man resumed his pacing while he smoked.

Olly sighed resignedly and glanced out of the window. He had to swallow his astonishment and curb any sudden excited movement. At all costs he must not alert his adversary to what he had just seen. Outside, under the street light, standing looking up at the guest house was a little group of people. Three people to be precise: Marc, Alicia and Adriana. They probably couldn't see him but he was sure it was them. Oliver recognized Marc's bright checked coat about which they had all teased him, likening it to a Canadian lumber jacket.

Oliver waited until the man was exactly opposite before making his move. Then, using his body as well as his tied hands, he violently shoved the table over towards the man. The gun and mobile slid to the floor with a crack. The gun had gone off as the heavy table crashed down on it, the bullet embedding itself somewhere in the surrounding wood furniture. The grey man leapt out of the way in surprise. As his opponent hesitated just for a moment, Oliver grabbed the fire extinguisher with both hands and, shouting at the top of his voice, thrust it with all the force that he could muster through the closed window. Glass flew everywhere and Olly felt blood coursing down his wrist and on one side of his face. He was vaguely aware of returning shouts from the street and a resounding bang from the exploding extinguisher outside.

There wasn't a moment to lose. He threw himself towards his adversary who was now swearing oaths and madly scrabbling beneath the table for the gun, which had slid further out of reach. Oliver now knew that the weapon was loaded: he had to stop the man from retrieving it. His hands were almost free and he could use his feet in their sturdy boots but he had to get around the upturned table. The Iranian had located the weapon once more and was stretching for it. Oliver dived just as the Iranian, half crouched, turned towards him with the gun and fired.

Outside, Adriana had caught just a glimpse of the man at the window and the voice had confirmed who she'd seen. It was Olly and he'd called her name. Alicia had run to enlist help from the café, but when Marc and Adriana heard the two shots they made for the door of the guest house. It was open, somebody on the ground floor had been sleeping in their room, awoken by the gunshots and noise outside. They had also come out to see what was going on. Adriana and Marc burst in.

"Entschuldigen sie, entschuldigen sie." They barged in and up the stairs, Marc in front.

"Second floor, end of the passage; quick follow me but stay behind," he shouted.

They reached the door, where there was now an unnerving silence from within.

"This is without doubt the right room, stand back, right back."

Marc threw his weight against the locked door, once, twice, three times to no avail; then Alicia arrived panting and they all went at it together.

"Ambulance and police are all on the way," she cried as the door creaked, gave and flew open, ripping the catch clean off the door frame.

It took a mere second to take in the dramatic scene before them. A strange foreign man was lying, half across the upturned table, badly wounded; his hand held to his stomach with blood pumping out between his fingers. Oliver was sitting propped against the far wall, with blood streaming down one side of his face, from a cut underneath his eye. His wrist was roughly bound up in what appeared to be a torn piece of bloodied curtain, which he must have ripped from the rail at the window.

"God Almighty! He's actually smiling. Here... hold that to the other one's stomach, he's out of it," Marc commanded, grabbing a towel off the bed and throwing it to Alicia as he rushed to Olly's side. "OK, let's have a look at you... Adriana get me something as clean as possible from the bathroom. Your face is fine Oliver," he said merely glancing at the cut before carefully unwinding the cloth from around Oliver's wrist. Adriana arrived at his side with another small linen towel and a blanket which she carefully put around Olly's shoulders.

"Olly, how are you feeling? Have you any pain elsewhere?" Oliver merely shook his head; he was unable to speak and his face was white but it still retained the semblance of a smile.

"You've lost a lot of blood, my friend. It's just missed the main artery by the looks of it. You'll live," pronounced Marc pleased with his findings.

"Just stay quiet where you are for the moment, take a few breaths for me... that's right, in, out, in and out..." He re-bound Oliver's arm, tightly, telling Adriana to take over and to loosen it when he told her to, while he checked the other man.

"I think Olly's going to pass out and he's shaking," whispered Alicia anxiously, as she watched from her position, crouching beside Marc while he examined the foreigner. He looked up instantly.

"It's the shock. Adriana," he called across softly, "keep him awake if you can, just continue talking and make him answer; we'll have more help in a minute." They already could hear the noise of police sirens approaching.

"Now let's see what I can do for this chap."

"How can you do anything to help him?" hissed Alicia.

Marc was unfazed.

"Because, no matter what he's done, this man is still a human being who needs medical help. He is seriously wounded and it is part of my training to save his life if I can. Also it is quite probable that he can tell us where Emma is. So, at all costs I don't want him dead," Marc finished severely.

Alicia, reprimanded and slightly ashamed, sat back on her haunches without answering. He was right of course. In her shocked state she'd let her emotions get the better of her.

The Iranian was in a lot of pain from the gunshot wound to his stomach, but compos mentis enough to cringe away from Marc as he knelt beside him. His doctor's instinct was all to the fore as he administered to this stranger who, most likely, was responsible for abducting his beloved wife.

"It's alright I am an English doctor, a doctor," Marc tried to explain gently to the wounded man, as he tried to stem the bleeding.

"It's *doktor*," a weak voice came from the other side of the room. "Doctor is *'doktor'* in Farsi, almost the same, and he'll understand if you pronounce it as I just did." Marc looked up and smiled in relief. A little colour was returning to Oliver's face.

"Good, alright. Adriana, loosen that dressing for a minute then tighten it again. Olly, let's have some more. What is 'don't worry, help is at hand'?"

Five minutes later the room was full, with another doctor, ambulance men and the police. Marc let the Swiss doctor with equipment take his place and then moved to the other side of the room to minister to Oliver. The girls stood in the corner out of the way while the professionals took charge.

"I think I'd better try and get hold of our two men," whispered Alicia, getting out her mobile and edging outside into the passage as the stretchers were manoeuvred expertly into the room. Adriana followed her out.

"Um, they are never going to believe how busy we have been. I just hope to God that they have found Emma."

"And what about Rose? Olly doesn't even know she's disappeared." Alicia hesitated before putting the call through. Adriana noticed that her hands were shaking: not surprising as there was a lot of blood around. She felt pretty shaky herself.

"We can't say a thing to Olly for the moment. The shock would be too much, but our men need to know." Alicia began to walk out of earshot, down the passage.

"Yes," muttered Adriana after her, "I'm very much afraid that they do need to know there is yet another person missing from our diminishing group."

❋ ❋ ❋

CHAPTER 24

"THERE'S a missed call from Alicia," Guy told Julian as the men re-emerged from the barn. "She wouldn't ring me without good reason. Zak: would you and a couple of men like to take these two down to Spiegelsee police station? I'll make this call and follow you down there."

One of the other policemen was busy answering his emergency bleeper. He stepped forward to tell Guy that there was an incident involving some English people taking place at present in the town near the station.

"Alright everybody, go! I'll be right behind you."

Guy tapped in Alicia's number. Both men waited, sensing that the two girls were likely to be in the middle of this latest commotion. She answered immediately.

"Alicia, what's going on, where are you?" Guy listened intently without speaking then:

"But you're all unhurt except for Olly. How is he?" He held the mobile away a little and Julian bent closer to hear as well.

"Right! Stay there. We're on our way."

"Fill me in quickly," Julian said. "I only heard half of it." Guy turned to his friend.

"The girls are fine. Olly is hurt with a bad cut to his wrist. He's lost a lot of blood but will be alright. He's on his way to the local hospital. Marc is with him. The Iranian boss is shot through the stomach and in a bad way. They think that with luck he'll live but he's being sent by helicopter to the hospital in Bern. They can't deal with this serious an injury in the valley and of course they'll want him there for interrogation, as soon as he's up to it. That's it, in a nutshell. The girls are waiting for us in Spiegelsee, in the café near the station. So... let's go."

They walked towards their snowmobile. Julian was grinning.

"Good old Olly. He got his grey man then."

"Yes, he certainly did. At some cost though, by the sound of it; and what the hell were the girls doing down there anyway? They were supposed to stay put in the hotel."

*

Emma and Rose were stretched out in front of the dying fire. After talking quietly through the early hours of the night they'd finally gone to sleep, tucked up, one on either end of the sofa, covered in rugs. Neither could be bothered to seek out the bedrooms although they knew that Steffi wouldn't have minded at all. She would have been delighted they were out of harm's way and to know that her house had become this safe haven. Emma was the first to stir. The leg she'd been lying on had also gone to sleep. She needed to stretch but didn't want to wake Rose who was facing the fire, with one hand dropped over the side resting on the back of their four-legged friend. He was also was out for the count.

Emma lay wiggling her toes, trying to ease her numb leg. It began to come to life again with uncomfortable prickling sensations, which made her want to giggle. Rose rolled over onto her back and opened one eye.

"Thank goodness, you're awake. I've got cramp and have to move. Ouch!" Emma cried getting off the sofa to move around and rub the back of her leg. The dog also woke and stood looking from one to the other, wagging his tail.

"What time is it?" asked Rose yawning.

"Early dawn I should think, it's beginning to get light. But I can't see my watch unless we light the lamp. I don't think that matters now, not any more. We are quite safe."

"Don't," replied Rose quickly. "There's no hurry, let's just lie here and consider things for a bit longer. Put another log on the fire." She turned over to face the fire again. Emma realized that Rose really was worried about getting into trouble on their return.

"You know, they are going to be so pleased to see us, Rose. Everything else will pale into total insignificance. You really don't need to be so anxious."

"I know, I know I'm just being stupid, but I feel a bit like I'm going to be facing the firing squad. Which I have to do... but let's not hurry too much, that's all."

Emma laughed. "Well, I'm going to make a cup of tea on the gas hob. I even found some long life milk. That will make you feel better. Then I suggest we have something to eat and make a plan of action after that. Alright?"

"Okay," replied Rose. "I'm going to the bathroom." She got up and shuffled off in the half light, wrapped in the rug which trailed along the floor behind her.

Emma put the dog out. It had stopped snowing and there was a pink glimmer of dawn rising steadily over the horizon. It was exceedingly cold away from the cosy fire. She pushed the door almost shut and went to boil the kettle. She had slept well considering the strange circumstances and couldn't wait now to be back with her husband and friends.

Rose re-appeared. The dog had come back in so she shut the door and returned to her place on the sofa.

"God, it's cold," she said, almost disappearing underneath the blanket. Emma handed her the tea and chucked another log on the fire. They sipped their tea in silence for a few moments.

"I realize I do sound seriously selfish. You must be desperate to get back to Marc and the others. I'm so sorry Emma. Are you still alright though, with the baby I mean? "

"Yes, I think all is well, so far at any rate and I feel fine, but don't worry; we'll go back when we're both ready. Guess what? I've found some cereal and some tinned cherries, so we'll have a feast first."

They washed, then ate breakfast and tided up as best they could. Emma penned a note for Steffi. Although they expected to see her, Emma felt that she should write down how she was feeling this morning, safe in Steffi's cosy farmhouse, after escaping so recently. Things would be different when she returned once more to normal life in the valley and she never wanted to forget this precious time she'd spent here with Rose.

Rose left her boots and skis propped tidily up against the wall, with a note stuck in the top of a boot. Then they went together to look for alternative clothing for Emma. Rose found suitable heavy walking footwear for herself. Emma should have the snow shoes.

Emma borrowed some warm boots, a thick jersey and an anorak with a hood. Then, after replacing the key carefully under the brick, the two girls set off together down the track, with the mountain dog leading the way.

There were no footprints. The snow lay deep everywhere, shaped into huge drifts up against the farm buildings where, through the night, the wind had gusted uninterrupted. The newly-risen sun was beginning to spread a warm glow across the landscape and the virgin snow glistened wherever the light touched.

"It's so beautiful up here, isn't it? Awe-inspiring almost, especially seeing it like this and having it all to ourselves."

"Yes," agreed Emma, letting out a long sigh and tucking her arm through Rose's. "It's more beautiful than I could possibly have imagined."

There was no rush. They couldn't hurry with Emma in her awkward snow shoes and Rose's feet disappearing with every step.

They halted awhile, to revel at the flawless silent vista spread before them; to both look and experience the rare, muffled quiet that the abundant blanketing of snow created. When the cold began to penetrate their warm clothing they moved on again, tramping slowly on through the thick carpet of soft white, their own breathing and their clumsy movements the only sound to be heard. Even the birds must have been resting and recovering after the violent storm.

The next time they stopped Rose attempted to send a text to Olly. After a while she saw the 'message sent' and so they were hopeful that, at last, it had at least partially got through.

❄

Zak had found Alicia and Adriana standing shivering in the doorway in a state of mild shock, watching the goings-on as the police moved in to begin sealing off the adjoining stairways and passageways of the guest house. The roads round about were also being closed and diversions put in place in advance of the early morning traffic. He had made it his business to extract the girls from the gory surroundings of the guest house and manoeuvre them into the café for a hot, sweet drink. He'd just caught a glimpse of Oliver being carried into the ambulance: Marc went with him. The helicopter, with the other seriously wounded patient, was already airborne and on it's way to Bern. It was beginning to get light and he saw the machine's black shape silhouetted against the dawn sky, the noise of the rotors diminishing as it turned away and flew off down the valley.

It had been a long and eventful night but, thought Zak apprehensively, they still hadn't located Emma and the girls had just told him about the disappearance of the other English girl Rose. Guy and Julian were going to be extremely unhappy about this latest development.

With Zak helping to translate, the police took statements from both Alicia and Adriana and also their fingerprints. When Julian and Guy walked in a short time later, the questioning had just finished and the girls were chatting to the senior police officer who, with several others, was sitting at a table close by. The café had been requisitioned, following the incident in the guest house, so that it could be used as a centre for the investigation. Everybody had a steaming hot cup of something and the woman responsible appeared to be delighted in the activity.

The men greeted the girls with a mixture of obvious disapproval at their presence, but delighted relief that they appeared to be relatively unscathed.

"I know that we shouldn't be here and all that," Alicia said in a rush and standing up, "but actually it was very lucky for Oliver that we were and... there's something else, important, that you need to know." She was looking directly at her husband, making sure that she

232

had his attention. She'd better get it over with and quickly. He was going to be furious. "I was going to tell you on the mobile but as you were coming straight here it seemed better to tell you in person."

Guy and Julian sat down and stared up at Alicia in wary silence, waiting for her to continue. It sounded serious. What on earth was this about? Alicia glanced at Adriana who merely nodded encouragement and stepped up closer beside her.

"Well... you see, the reason we were all here in the first place was because we were looking for Rose." Alicia fixed her gaze once more on her husband. "I'm afraid to have to tell you that she's also disappeared." There was a deadly hush around the table. Guy's blue eyes blazed. He stood up, almost knocking the chair over.

"Disappeared, disappeared! What on earth do you mean disappeared? Rose was with you at the hotel." He sounded furious, particularly because he must be so tired, thought Adriana chipping in.

"It's nobody's fault Guy. Rose just took off without saying anything to any of us. I'm afraid it was out of our control."

"But where the hell did she think she was going?" asked Julian, "The weather's been appalling." The men sat looking astonished, waiting for answers.

"We think she went up the mountain, to Steffi's summer farmhouse, to look for Steffi's dog."

"To look for Steffi's dog? To search for a dog? Are you serious? In these conditions for God's sake? She must be out of her mind. She can't have been so stupid! I don't believe this!" he finished shaking his head in disbelief.

'Oh hell! He really is livid,' thought Alicia unhappily. "Alright, if you'd just listen a minute, I'll tell you what we have found out so far, but first please tell us: is there any news of Emma? We are desperate to know, as is poor Marc, although at the moment he's caught up in looking after his patient."

Guy recounted all that they had learned about Emma's likely escape on the tractor. The girls were, unsurprisingly, amazed at the story he had to tell. Julian went out for a cigarette. The young women organized more hot drinks and something to eat for the men before Alicia began their own tale of events. The men checked their mobiles once more hoping that perhaps at last there might be some news. Guy was still thoroughly enraged by Rose's thoughtless disappearance at such an inopportune moment. He appeared a little more than irritated, but at least he was sitting drinking hot coffee and eating a sandwich, while he fiddled with his phone.

"This area has to have the very worst mobile reception anywhere," he muttered crossly, stuffing the offending instrument back in his pocket. "Almost impossible, even for tracking purposes. Zak, can you get through to the hospital on the main line from the box in the square and get hold of Marc? Ask him to check his mobile for messages or missed calls and find out how Olly is faring. Tell him that all three Iranians are out of action and that although we haven't yet found Emma the situation looks promising. Then come back here. Meanwhile, I want to hear what Alicia and Adriana have to say. Then we'll assess the situation regarding the second missing person and after everybody has had a short rest we'll get back up the mountain." Zak rose from his chair and put on his coat ready to leave. Guy glanced at his watch.

"Five forty-five. Emma's been gone nearly thirty-six long hours: too long," he muttered, tiredly passing his hands across his eyes. "It will soon be fully light which will make things a lot easier. Thanks Zak. Can you also get us a weather forecast? Judging from that sky, it looks hopeful. Please report back as soon as the search team is assembled."

Adriana and Alicia were winding up their own story when Zak re-appeared. The good news was that Oliver was all stitched up and recovering, although required to stay in hospital for a few more hours as he'd lost a lot of blood. Marc also had said that he was sorry to say that he'd received no enlightening text and that he himself would shortly be on his way back.

"What about Olly's phone?" Julian asked quietly. There was dead silence as they all stopped talking to look at him. "Well... he had one didn't he?"

"Shit! Of course you're right. It could be anywhere and there could easily be a message from Rose. As it is I have a strange feeling about Rose's possible whereabouts."

Guy paused for a mere moment. Then, "Zak, get on to Bern and ask them to check the grey man's clothes. Then make sure that the local hospital gives Marc the basic medical supplies to bring back to us, especially the thermal gear. Julian, ask the police to look in the jeep and also find out if they found a second phone in the room and if so to bring it here. If there's no sign, check again. I want Olly's mobile. I need to haul off the army and to quickly reorganize the search for today. Also inform the powers that be that there will be no nine o'clock telephone call from the Iranians to wait for. Thankfully, they are now all under arrest."

Alicia and Adriana sat watching with interest. They realized that, although exhausted, the two men wouldn't rest until both Emma and Rose were found safe. They became different people when they were working on a job, so the girls kept quiet waiting to see what would happen next. The police were busy making their own reports and sorting out the segregation of the room in the guest house. There were a few people in residence at the time of the crisis and luckily all on the lower floor. They had appeared out of the building, blinking in the bright lights, wondering what on earth was going on. All of them had been reassured and escorted back to their rooms.

"When Marc returns, the girls can go to the hotel with him," Julian suggested.

"No," Alicia interrupted. "No way: if the situation is no longer dangerous we are coming to help look for Emma and Rose, aren't we Ari?" Adriana nodded enthusiastically. "We're not going to be left out this time," Alicia finished determinedly.

"And Marc is bound to want to come too," Adriana added for good measure.

Guy and Julian looked at each other. For the first time since entering the room Guy lowered his professional guard just long enough to allow himself the flickering suggestion of a smile in answer to the girls' defiance. Julian, covering his face with his hands, got up from the chair.

"Oh my Lord. I'm going out for a cigarette," he said, kissing the top of his girlfriend's head in passing.

"Alright," said Guy, lowering his eyes to hide his amusement, "but you'll stay behind us with Marc in case you hold us up. Please make sure you're both dressed warmly enough. As soon as I hear about the mobile, we're on our way. Emma has been out there a long time and she could be hurt, or at least very cold and wet."

"Exactly," replied Alicia matching her husband's tone, "and Marc's not just married to Emma, he's a doctor and a bloody good one at that. We've seen him in action, haven't we Ari?" Alicia looked again across to her friend for confirmation.

"We certainly have," answered Adriana. "We most certainly have."

✻　✻　✻

CHAPTER 25

OLIVER lay in his bed at the hospital, staring at the ceiling and smiling. He preferred to think himself elsewhere. He wasn't good at being still for long periods, but presently life wasn't quite normal. He didn't like the medical smell or the fact that he was supposedly unable to do much for himself for the moment. So he repeatedly decided to re-live the whole drama, particularly the bit when the grey man had actually managed to shoot himself in the stomach with his own gun. The trouble was that Olly kept going to sleep just before he got to the final showdown. Anyway, it didn't really matter because every time he woke up he remembered all over again that he had got the better of the Iranian. He hadn't let the other two down after all and this was of the utmost importance to him.

Carrying the required equipment, Marc had just left the hospital to rejoin the others. Olly was very disappointed that he couldn't go too. He wanted to be there when they found Emma. Wherever had she got to? Marc had updated him with the news of Emma's escape on a tractor, of all things, and in such an extraordinary manner. Also he told him that all the Iranian henchmen were now in a secure place under guard. This was brilliant news. The danger was over, but he didn't like missing out on the winding up of the operation.

Now Oliver couldn't wait to see his girlfriend, but Marc and the Swiss doctor insisted that he had to stay put for a bit longer. He really did love Rose very much and now he knew for certain that he wanted to marry her.

Perhaps he'd ask her when she came in to see him. He could ask one of the nurses to get him a rose. Yes, that was a good idea, he thought. It wouldn't matter what colour. Any rose would do. He could practice what he was going to say beforehand, while he was submerged in this strange state of enforced and lethargic euphoria.

The morphine, which they'd given him for the pain, did muddle his thoughts and make him dream. He felt a bit as though he was on another planet: rather similar to a hangover but thankfully without the queasiness. He couldn't see or feel the wound on his wrist, it was well bandaged, but he was vaguely aware of the stitches to the cut on his face. He could see them if he looked down, sticking up like a set of cat's whiskers. Marc had said he might have a slight James Bond-ish looking scar under the eye. Oliver rather liked the idea of that. Rose would be proud of him and so would his parents. Smiling happily, he began to practice his proposal. There was a dark girl approaching his bed at this very moment. Good. It was probably Rose, but, oh dear, what a nuisance! He thought he might have to go to sleep again before she reached him.

*

Rose stopped: her mobile was vibrating in her pocket. She tried to put a call through to the number which kept trying to reach her, but still it wouldn't connect.

"There's a message come in... hang on it's fragmented; there's still no proper reception. I suppose those mast things are in some way blocked in certain positions by the overhanging mountains; let's see... it says: 'On our way... we're on our way...' the rest hasn't come through yet. That's a very unlike-Olly message. It's his number but it's strange, because he always sends me a flower at the end and usually a rose. Oh God! Emma, I really am in trouble. Anyway they know roughly where we are from my text, which obviously got through, so we're bound to bump into them if we keep to the main track. Are you alright Emma?"

"Yes, unless we meet the other lot."

"We won't. I'm sure they've legged it. After all they lost you, had no idea where you'd gone and wouldn't have hung around looking for you in that appalling weather. Also we are in touch with our other halves now, so I'm sure it won't be long before we see or hear them coming up to meet us."

"I suppose you're right and we've got Trost to protect us." The dog looked up and wagged his tail as if in agreement. "However, nobody is ever going to take me a prisoner again. I have some weaponry in my pocket, just in case." Emma rummaged around in her pocket and pulled out a tenderizing meat hammer and a lethal looking kitchen knife in a protective cover, both of which she'd borrowed from Steffi.

"God almighty! I should think your captors would run a mile if they saw us coming with those." Rose was laughing, but she realized that Emma was quite serious and that she would have no qualms about using either weapon if she needed to.

"By the way, what exactly does 'Trost' mean?" Emma asked as she bent to stroke his head. "I meant to ask you back in the house. Do you know?"

"Well, you're not going to believe it but strangely enough I think it means comfort... or something like that anyway."

Emma looked up at her new friend, eyes wide with surprise.

"Well I thought perhaps it meant trust. How appropriate is that?"

"You were meant to meet... a higher power and all that," replied Rose, patting the dog and setting off once more. "Come on then. I don't want you getting cold again, not in your state," she flung back over her shoulder, giggling.

"Bossy too," muttered Emma, following obediently.

＊

Julian and Guy set off up the mountain track once more, with a fleet of snowmobiles following. Marc and Adriana were immediately behind, then Alicia and Zak with a four-man police escort bringing up the rear. The noise of the machines bouncing across the snow shattered the still white silence. They even had a loud speaker, to help with the search. If necessary their voices would reach down into the deepest valleys, between the mountains. They stopped when they came to the farm with the broken door. Zak stood, taking in the scene of Emma's obvious incarceration. He bent to inspect the ground at the entrance, kicking the snow away and uncovering the rough tractor ruts. He straightened up muttering, shaking his head in disbelief, then turned to the others with a grin.

"The tractor had a plough attached... look here at the width of these tracks." Zak walked back and forth across the rough surface, shovelling away the snow with a broken piece of wood, and revealing the evidence where a massive machine had hacked up the earth as it turned.

They all stared down to where he was pointing at the clearly defined furrows, perfectly preserved in the frozen ground.

"How do you know these ruts are recent?" asked Alicia puzzled.

"Because inside the barn, where it's not so cold, the mud along the same indentations is still relatively soft and all this broken wood confirms Guy and Julian's previous findings. Emma escaped not only on a tractor, but it had a plough attached behind it. She wouldn't have known how to release it."

"But where on earth did she go? How could she disappear on that?"

Zak continued with his theory.

"Emma is an intelligent lady. I think she has been here in the summer as well. On escaping she probably recognized where she was; but she knew that, although easier in every respect, she might meet her captors if she headed downhill towards the village and they, of course, had also gone that way. So she did the opposite, the unexpected. She went up the mountain instead." Zak stood pointing the way ahead.

Silently, they all turned to follow his gaze and to listen. There was nothing. Not a sound or a sign of anything: just a vast white silence and a sparkling blanket of pure new snow covering the entire area.

Guy turned to survey the group spread around him. All of them were looking up the mountain, their thoughts of one mind, he was sure: deep admiration for this gutsy young Englishwoman for whom they were all searching. It was a strange moment and one he would always remember, all of them striving towards the same end: Emma's safe recovery.

Then Guy began scraping more of the snow away to expose additional marks. Sure enough they were curving uphill.

"You're right Zak. What an amazingly intrepid woman your wife must be, Marc." He walked across to where the doctor was standing still gazing further up the mountain.

"Yes, but where the hell is she now?"

"Don't you worry we know she's up there. We'll find her. We also know from the few words of fragmented text, when we found Olly's phone, that Rose is also in the land of the living. We'll find them both. Zak, will you please touch base with your people who are coming in from the top of the lift? Also, check with those at the bottom of the run and at the train station. I'll ring the hotel. It's fully light now and Rose may well have managed to ski down from wherever she found shelter."

Adriana, Alicia and Marc talked quietly together and drank hot coffee from the flasks the café had given them, while the other men went about their business, coordinating the search party.

The sun was up and the light crept steadily on, across the landscape, melting the shadows as it rose above the mountain tops and began to reach into the hidden valleys. The early morning visitors felt the warmth on their faces and the two figures trudging unknowingly downhill towards them felt it on their backs. It was a good, positive feeling for all concerned.

The search party resumed their trek up towards Steffi's farm. Halfway there, they came out from the trees to see two dark figures and a dog, starkly silhouetted against the mountain slope above, slipping and sliding down towards them. Julian took out the binoculars while the others all held their breath.

"It's definitely two women and a large mountain dog. They've taken a short cut off the track. It's too far to see their faces. The sun's behind them and in my eyes. I think, believe it or not, that it's both our missing girls. Listen." He held up his hand.

They strained their ears to hear. An eagle flew high above, eerily calling to its mate, swooping and gliding in the thermals, distracting them momentarily. Then, another sound began to filter through. Women's laughter – as with difficulty the two people continued to wade slowly downwards through the deep snow. Then they too stopped, suddenly and warily moving to stand closely together, shading their eyes against the glare, surveying the stationary group of people waiting, so obviously, to waylay them far below.

They're frightened, poor darlings, thought Guy. They looked as startled as deer, standing so small and vulnerable against the great white backdrop. He quickly took the loud speaker from Julian and cleared his throat.

"They can't be sure that it's us: everybody wave like mad." He put the speaker to his mouth.

"Emma, Rose, it's us. It's alright, we're here, you're safe, quite safe, you're safe."

The echo wound its way around the valley, 'you're safe... quite safe... you're safe... safe... safe'.

The two small shapes remained still for a fraction in time, until the echoing words reached them. Then they waved frantically in return and began literally to tumble down the slope together. The search party started their machines and sped off to meet them at the bottom of the incline.

Marc's heart was hammering with excitement but he would not let himself believe that this nightmare was finally over until he had his wife securely in his arms again. He could recognize her familiar figure now, even in her unusual clothing and he could hear her voice calling to him.

Rose was desperately trying to make out on which machine Olly was riding; she could see the girls, Julian and now Guy and also Marc. But where was Olly? The other man riding pillion with Alicia was a stranger, as were the four men following. Oh my God! Where was Olly? He was missing from the party, which could only mean one thing... All she had thought about throughout the whole drama was herself, quite unthinking of the danger he was in. He was obviously either seriously wounded or killed or he would have been here. This horrendous likelihood had never occurred to her in all the time that he'd been away. She'd been too busy being cross and doing her own thing. How could she have been so selfish when he had set out so willingly to help the other two men search for Emma?

Alicia watched as Emma, in the awkward snow shoes, scrambled carefully down the rest of the slope and Marc hastened to meet her. It reminded her of another time, another place, a different couple and a different situation. She leant out from behind Zak's broad back to catch her husband's eye. Still sitting astride his machine, he was turned around and smiling back at her.

Adriana averted her eyes as Marc and Emma came together, to allow them at least a little privacy. Then she saw Rose, standing stock still and looking down on them all, a distraught expression on her face. And Adriana immediately understood. Oliver wasn't here and Rose imagined the worst. Of course she would. Adriana leapt off the machine, nearly knocking it over and began making her way across the drifts to where Rose was standing in stricken silence.

"Rose... Rose! It's OK... Olly's alive, he's alright, I promise you." Adriana arrived at Rose's side and grabbing her by the shoulders turned her around to face her. Rose seemed not to hear and wouldn't look at

Adriana. All she could think about was that she'd lost Olly. She began to shake. Her chin was already quivering and her normally sparkling eyes had a faraway, vacant appearance. Adriana shook her, roughly.

"Rose, look at me; listen to me. Olly is alive and kicking. He's been hurt a little and is in hospital but he'll be fine." Rose blinked as she began to absorb this information and her face became alert again: like the sun coming out from behind a cloud, out of the dark and into the light, thought Adriana fleetingly. Rose opened her mouth to speak and promptly burst into tears. Adriana held the sobbing girl and continued to reassure her.

"Rose! It's alright… really it is and what's more… actually Olly's turned into a bit of a hero as well. You can be really proud of him. We all are."

❆   ❆   ❆

CHAPTER 26

EFFICIENT, fully equipped and ready for anything, two Swiss Alpine police removed the short skis strapped to their backs, slid their feet into place, clicked the bindings shut and then expertly set off down the mountain, gladly giving up their seats on the snow machines to the two exhausted girls. They all watched in awe as the two retreating figures skimmed over the snow drifts, twisting and jumping over the lumps and bumps and then, in a flash they were gone; disappeared through the trees.

"It's alright for some," remarked Guy, chuckling "makes our skiing look a bit pathetic though, don't you think Julian?"

"Speak for yourself," Julian replied grinning like a Cheshire cat.

"Alright everybody. Mount up. It's time to go home and 'don't spare the horses'. These girls need a hot bath." Understandably, everyone was euphoric at finding both women together and relatively unscathed.

Rose and Emma had started down the mountain at dawn that morning and had been struggling through the heavy snow for almost four hours. They were both beginning to feel cold, now that they'd stopped walking. Thermal blankets were unpacked and wrapped around them and Guy insisted on each being given a quaff of some powerful alcoholic drink to warm them up, before setting off speedily once more, down the track. Guy wanted the girls, Emma in particular, to return quickly to the welcoming warmth of the hotel and to hear her story. Only then would he finally feel able to relax.

Emma, slightly squiffy because the alcohol had gone straight to her head, was hanging on behind Marc, giggling weakly.

"Don't go too fast, I'm a bit fragile and I want to make sure that Steffi's dog keeps up with us. Trost, here boy… here, come follow us now! What on earth was in that flask? I'm feeling quite away with the fairies."

"It will do you good and keep you warm until we get back," Marc shouted back over his shoulder, "just hang on tight, that's all. Today is the first time I've driven one of these things. I won't go too fast, but they're not that easy," he muttered, trying to prevent tipping his passenger off as they negotiated another mound of snow which, in the wind that had got up, had drifted unhelpfully across the track.

Trost floundered along behind them, with Emma constantly turning around to see that he was following, calling him encouragingly. The dog had no intention of being left behind and was surprisingly agile in the deep snow.

Guy and Julian left the girls at the hotel with Marc to look after them, while they reported to their police base in town. Later, after lunch, they would all go down to the hospital to see Olly and hopefully bring him back with them.

Marc saw Rose to her room, after reassuring her yet again that Olly was going to be soon recovered. Then he went to run a bath for his wife.

He poured a liberal amount of sweet orange and healing lavender oil into the bath water. He'd brought it for her from a trip to Greece. Emma was sitting on a towel on the bed, looking slightly dazed, now that it was all over.

"My legs feel a bit wonky."

"I'm not in the least surprised. Let's get you into the bath and then bed for a bit. I think you should have a rest before lunch: we can have it sent up if you like."

"No way! I shall be starving by then. I'd rather go down and I want to see Hélène as well."

"Yes alright, Hélène's been wonderful throughout, but first let's get these wet things off." He began to pull off her trousers. "God, I can't wait to get you tucked up in that bed." He looked up at Emma, who bent to ruffle his hair, unable to speak. She put her arms around her husband and clung to him.

"Come, my darling it's alright, it's all over now and I'm going to carry you to that bath." His face was wet from his own tears as well as hers. He lifted her gently, then helped her get into the warm fragrant water.

"Sorry," was all Emma could manage. She was shaking with emotion. Marc sat beside her and taking the sponge began to lovingly wipe her face.

"There's nothing to be sorry about. You're wonderful. I always knew that you were an exceptional person, strong and so brave. You're clever, so much fun, totally selfless, soft, warm and… fantastically sexy. I just love you so much and can't believe that I now have you back safe. I was getting pretty desperate; although I had to keep it together for the others' sakes. I wouldn't have been able to cope if anything had happened to you." He bent his head to nuzzle the back of her neck, with both arms around her, holding her shoulders. Emma was crying openly now.

"Have a good cry my darling. It's good for you," Marc said, pulling himself together and continuing to wash her. "All is well now: I'll rinse your hair while you have a good soak, then you must get out and get dry."

Emma still couldn't speak but she did as he asked, turned and moved around while he dried her and put her arms into the towelling robe that he held for her. Then he picked her up again and carried her to the bed. Emma was still crying quietly. The doctor knew it to be just reaction but the shaking had stopped and he was satisfied that his wife, miraculously, was suffering no serious ill effects. He had checked her thoroughly as he'd bathed her, especially the bump on her head. He would take her to the hospital tomorrow for a scan, just to be on the safe side. Now she was exhausted and needed to sleep.

It wasn't until they were safely tucked up in bed together that she was able to tell him. Marc didn't hear her properly at first because, still so emotional, she had mumbled her words into his chest. He propped himself up on one elbow and looking down at her tenderly, asked her to repeat what she had just said. Emma raised her bright eyes to his. They locked and a smile spread slowly across her face.

"I have a secret. It's a very special secret that through these last horrific hours, together with a picture of you in my head, has kept me sane and sensible." Marc raised a quizzical eyebrow. She nodded.

"Yes. As a doctor you'll know about these things, but I think that perhaps we should be a little careful as, all being well and in spite of everything, believe it or not we're going to have a baby." Astonished and speechless Marc stared down at his brave little wife. Then the emotion overcame him too and he also burst into tears.

Never had he felt so protective. Their love had given her the strength she'd needed against all odds to escape and survive whilst carrying his child. He kissed her warm, scented body and stroked her tenderly until the bad memories began to recede in her mind. The tears stopped finally. Emma couldn't think of anything else but how much she loved this man she might never have seen again, had the unthinkable happened. At this time the drama through which she'd just lived paled into insignificance besides the power of their feelings for each other.

Another time and another place came to their minds. They'd once made love in the cool shade of some olive trees, with the lingering perfume of orange blossom drifting in the air. This time it was gentle and different, but just as sweet.

Holding his wife as if he'd never let her go again, both exhausted people then sank into a deep, contented sleep. Emma dreamt of walking from a cold, dark place and then out into the warm shining light once more. When she awoke the feeling of well-being remained. Her world had shifted on its axis, spiralled out of control and then settled itself again. All was well and everything once more was in its rightful place.

On the coldest night of the year she had fought for her life and that of her child and against all odds she had triumphed.

✳

Later, the others went together to see Olly in hospital. Rose couldn't wait. She'd had a bath and a quick bite to eat, but she was only interested in getting him back to the hotel where she could look after him. She was met by the doctor in charge and a senior nurse, who explained about the wound to Oliver's arm, the cut under his eye and that the drugs which they'd given him for the pain might make him seem a little strange.

"You mustn't worry," the doctor said in good English, "it's normal, but I think he wants to ask you something important." She winked at Rose. "He won't remember, but he's already asked the same question of three of my dark-haired staff." The doctor appeared thoroughly amused. "It is only the morphine; he gets a bit muddled and thought each of them was you. We'll give you a few minutes and then come to see you both before you take him home." They walked away smiling knowingly at each other. Rose was puzzled and the others looked at their feet.

"You see him first. Go on. We'll follow in a minute," Alicia ordered, giving Rose a push.

Oliver was lying in bed, looking really funny, pink-cheeked and pleased with himself. He had a red rose stuck between his teeth.

Rose arrived at his bedside, grinning.

"Hello Olly. Whatever are you doing?" she asked bending over to kiss him on the undamaged side of his face, trying to avoid both his stitches and getting poked in the eye by the rose. He was so sweet.

It was definitely her this time, thought Oliver. He could smell her scent, so he'd better get it over with quickly.

"Well I want to ask you to marry me, actually," he mumbled.

"What did you say?" She took the rose out of his mouth. Luckily someone had thought to take off all the prickly bits.

"I've been trying to get up the courage to ask you to marry me," he said clearly this time, "but it's been a bit difficult, because on this morphine stuff I kept going to sleep whenever you came in."

Rose opened her mouth to speak and then thought better of it. He was staring at her desperately, waiting for her answer.

"Oh Olly, of course I'll marry you." She put her head on his chest and grabbed hold of his free hand.

"I was rather hoping that you'd ask me and I've been so anxious. I thought that something dreadful had happened to you and that I might have lost you for good."

"Lost me? Good heavens no. The grey man wasn't going to get the better of me. How is he by the way?" Rose appeared nonplussed.

"Grey man, what grey man? What are you talking about, Olly?"

"Oh! Never mind. You obviously don't know the whole story yet. I'll fill you in later. But will you?"

"Will I what?"

"Marry me, of course." Rose laughed out loud.

"Of course I will marry you Olly. What a silly question when you already know the answer."

"Good, that's fixed then," said Oliver, triumphant and somewhat relieved that this huge matter was now resolved. "Where are the others? Let's tell them. You didn't come alone did you?" Rose shook her head.

"No, they're outside the door. I'll get them. Hang on." She bent to kiss his mouth then, holding the rose and beaming from ear to ear, she went to let the others in.

✳

Oliver was allowed to go back to the hotel as long as he went straight to bed for the rest of the afternoon. The others were all happy to rest up and recover from all the drama. With no sleep the night before, it had been a long day. They would meet in the bar before dinner. Olly too, if he felt up to it, by the evening.

The mood in the bar that night was one of immense relief and noisy elation. Hélène and her family saw to it that all the hotel guests were included and given a glass of champagne on the house. Oliver sat in the corner of the banquette seating, propped up on some cushions, thoroughly enjoying his 'heroic' image, although a little unhappy that Rose would only allow him the odd sip of the celebratory drink. However, he soon devised a method of persuading the barman to fill his glass up when Rose wasn't looking. Everybody had their part of the story to tell and it took some time to relate. Zak arrived to join them for dinner with Steffi and her lovely dog Trost. The dog went straight to Emma, giving Rose a slobbery lick on the way past, and Steffi hugged them both with tears streaming down her face.

"*Mein Gott,* thank goodness you're here safe. Thank goodness," was all she could manage.

Zak brought with him the latest news and three identical carrier bags as presents for the girls.

"What on earth is in it?" asked Alicia, taking hers, as he handed them around. They all opened them together and each pulled out an identical grey duffle coat. There was a moment's surprise then everybody burst into laughter.

"These are for three beautiful women to make sure..." Zak paused, waiting to be heard, then he looked purposely across at Emma before continuing grinning from ear to ear, "that they are properly clothed when next they go walking in these mountains on... the coldest night of the year." This brought the house down while Hélène and her husband, Anton, brought more champagne.

The soft-spoken Persian scientist and his brother had been given political asylum, provided that they agreed to divulge their knowledge. The two Iranian henchmen were to be sent back to Iran on the condition that the scientist's immediate family were first sent to Switzerland in exchange.

"And my grey man?" interrupted Olly desperate to know his assailant's fate. Zak smiled.

"Your grey man lives. He is still unconscious and will be immobile for some time to come. When he is able, he also will have to give information and then will be sent back to Iran as well, to face his fate there."

They were all quiet for a moment as they thought about what that fate might be. Then Guy broke the silence. It was over. The future of the men being returned to Iran was not for them to worry about.

"Alright everybody, dinner before the chef gives up on us!"

Everybody made their way to the dining room where a superb dinner of meat and fish fondu had been arranged. Zak, in fine form, regaled the whole dining room with hilarious accounts of some of his past exploits with Julian and Guy, who chipped in whenever he forgot something. Later, when Olly went to sleep at the table, the other men helped carry him upstairs.

Alicia and Guy were the last to go up to their room. She put her hand to her husband's cheek as he bent to unlock their door.

"Hang on, I think Ari has my mobile, I'd better retrieve it now, or it might wake them in the middle of the night. It might not be turned off. I won't be a minute."

"Alright but don't be too long," he answered with a twinkle, anticipating having his wife all to himself for a change. It seemed a long time ago since he'd had her warm welcoming body snuggled up beside him.

Alicia was just about to knock, when she realized that the door was slightly ajar. She listened before entering. She didn't want to interrupt anything. She could just hear their voices over the far side of the room and peeped in; they were on the balcony.

"I've been meaning to ask you something for a long time," Julian was standing with his back to the room and Adriana also was looking out into the starry night.

"Oh yes! And what could that be that's taken so long in the asking?"

Alicia felt her mouth quivering and she was trying hard not to burst out into happy laughter.

"At last. Thank God for that," she murmured to herself, as she melted into the background, closed the door quietly and went back along the passage to her own room, to tell her husband behind their own closed door. She couldn't wait to have his strong arms around her again. But Guy was stretched out across their bed, fully clothed and fast asleep. Alicia smiled down on him as she gently covered him with a spare blanket. Thanks mostly to this remarkable man and his team, they were all together and safe once more. All was well.

Tomorrow would be another day – and it would be more wonderful than any of them could possibly have imagined.

❊ ❊ ❊

'UNDER THE OLIVES'

ISBN 978-0-9563366-0-6

EMMA Brook, vulnerable and fragile, leaves a bad situation behind in England to explore the possibilities of a painting holiday in Greece for her 'Island Hops' travel Agency.

Underneath the olives Emma does indeed discover a whole secret world, just as the stranger on the plane implied. Who was the shy goatherd who never came out into the light? Why was he hiding? Who was the beautiful reclusive woman? And who were the mysterious little gypsies playing amongst the trees?

At the Hotel Stavros Emma meets an intriguing mix of diverse, irrevocably linked characters. In the hypnotic atmosphere of the olive grove she encounters tenderness, tragedy and unexpected drama. She finds the answer to a gripping riddle from the past and a certain magic for herself never before experienced.

�֍

Published by
Feel Good Books

'THE SMILE' 2008

ISBN 978-1-4251-7153-7

TWO women are thrown together through force of circumstance far beyond their control. With courage and determination they set forth to find out the truth and the whereabouts of the two men in their lives, suddenly disappeared, without trace, into thin air.

An unlikely boating accident in the South of France. A macabre funeral in Scotland. Unexpected and erotic happenings in Venice on the night of 'La Senza', the celebration of that city's marriage to the sea and a final, dramatic, scene on the island of Torcello, played out under the hot Italian sun.

※

Published by
Feel Good Books

For more information visit

Ginny Vere Nicoll's website

www.feelgoodbooksonline.com

Songs:
The Smile
Under the Olives
The Coldest Night of the Year

TOBIAH UK

www.tobiahuk.com

About The Author

GINNY Vere Nicoll was educated in England. After leaving school she attended art college. More recently she studied fine art at both West Dean College and privately in Italy. She exhibited successfully, in the West End of London, before turning her hand to writing.

Ginny has a large family and lives in an old farmhouse in West Sussex. Here, a few years ago, when the children were no longer so time consuming, Ginny began her books.

Passionate about travelling, particularly across Europe, either by car, train, or even by foot, Ginny takes every opportunity to collect information and material. 'The Coldest Night Of The Year', her third novel, set in Switzerland, completes the 'feel good' trilogy. Her first book, 'The Smile' is based in Europe, mostly in Italy, and her second, 'Under The Olives', evolves in the Ionian islands of Greece. There is a subtle link between the three stories when the charismatic characters meet up again and indulge in unexpected, action-packed holidays in stunning locations.

"I am an eternal optimist and romantic, writing is another life into which I escape from the real world. I strive to introduce you to my fictional characters and to take you to the imagined places in the hope that you will enjoy the feel good experience."

❋ ❋ ❋